READY OR NOT

A SUMMER NOVELLA

THE NAPE SERIES

BOOK 1

OLIVE WINTER

Author's Note: This is a work of fiction. All names, characters, places and events in this novel are a product of the author's imagination unless mentioned in the book's glossary. Locals and public names are sometimes used for atmospheric purposes. Any similarity to actual persons, living or dead, events, businesses, or institutions is purely coincidental.

Editing by Tasha L. Harrison
Cover Art by Celeste

ISBN 978-1-968974-01-5

CONTENTS

BOOK PLAYLIST

One Love - Cleo Sol
Here We Go (Uh Oh) - Coco Jones
Slow (Ft. Anaís Cardot) - Wiz Kid
4 Kampé II - Joé Dwèt Filé & Burna Boy
Baile Inolvidable - Bad Bunny
La Melodia - Putumayo & Guashara
When I'm In Your Arms - Cleo Sol
Sideways - Cleo Sol
Mood - Dvsn
Worst Behavior - Kwn
Same Mistake - Destin Conrad & Alex Isley
Why- Sasha Keable
Teach Me How To Love - Galdive
Best of Me - Anthony Hamilton
Ready or Not - After 7

Available on Spotify & Apple Music

This book is for the ones who've never known love,
but believe in it anyway.
The ones who keep showing up, even when life answers with the wrong names.

GLOSSARY + DICKTIONARY

Here's a list of things to better your reading experience as you're reading *Ready or Not*, Book one of the Nape Series.

Name pronunciation & their meanings:

Solène: (sɔ.lɛn/So-LENN) Latin origin, meaning "sun" or "solar," or it can be of French origin meaning "solemn".

Desiderio: (de.zi'dɛ.rjo/deh-zee-DEH-ree-oh) Latin origin meaning "yearning," "sorrow," or "desired".

Dick-tionary: **for those who want to skip straight to the smut during a reread or skip it over while reading b/c it's not your thing.*

Chapters Eleven + Twelve

What Things Mean:

Abuela – *Grandmother.*
Ay mami – *Oh, mama.*
Cabrón – *Bastard / A**hole / Badass.*
Calmate – *Calm down.*
Carajo – *Damn / Hell.*
Dios, ayúdame – *God, help me.*
Dios mío – *My God.*

Fantasmas – *Ghosts.* Supernatural entities or spirits of the dead.

Gracias, Madre Mía – *Thank you, my Holy Mother.*

La Melodía – *The Melody.* Refers to a musical tune, or metaphorically to something poetic or emotionally resonant.

Mierda – *Shit / Crap.*

Mírate, tan hermosa cuando estás así – *Look at you, so beautiful when you're like this.*

Pendejo – *Idiot / Dumbass.*

Perra – *Bitch.*

Te sientes mejor de lo que yo imaginé – *You feel better than I imagined.*

Vato – *Dude / Guy.*

Places in NYC that actually exist:

Empanada Mama: Yes they do sell the empanadas mentioned in the book. My favorite is the one that Solène selects.

Elsie's Rooftop: A rooftop lounge on Broadway

EverydayPPL: A live music event experience and culture platform hosted in multiple cities

DISCLAIMER

This is a work of **fiction**. While Desi might be the Dominican man of your wildest Bronx dreams, don't go expecting *every* Dominican guy be like him. Reality check: Too many can't even text back b/c they're too evil & they will have you outside their homes with a boom box looking like a fool after giving you the best D of your life!

Also, beware: this book contains steamy scenes and some alcohol references to make you want a cocktail *and* a cold shower. If you start swooning uncontrollably, fainting, or trying to call Desi, don't blame me—I warned you. Proceed with a fan, a drink, and a sense of humor.

1 / SOLÈNE

"IT'S TOO FUCKING hot outside for anyone to be smelling like a can of bounce that ass," Penelope said as she approached the rest of us with a stank look on her face. "This place is too packed for that."

"Who pissed you off?" Naomi asked. The sunshine brought out the warmth in her walnut skin tone as she lowered her Loewe square sunglasses to peek around the sea of people, searching for the root of Penelope's foul mood.

"Homeboy over there in the sky blue shirt sweating like hell done its big one on him." Using her lips, she motioned in the perpetrator's direction as she took a seat next to me on the rooftop's faux-leather grey couch. "I could smell him before he tried to talk to me."

"The one with that weird ass orangey-brown drink in his hand?" Naomi kept looking around. I followed her gaze and immediately spotted a burly, short Black man leaning against the bar that Penelope had been talking about—his shirt drenched in so much sweat that it practically clung to his skin. His dark hair clung to his forehead, and he seemed totally unaware of the damp patches spreading across his chest from his armpits. As if drawn by our side-eyes, he turned his head in our direction, revealing a patchy beard that even Jesus couldn't revive from the dead and we all shrieked.

"Oh my." My body shuddered again. "That man's marinating, and it's not even *that* hot."

Naomi let out a loud cackle, causing a couple of heads to turn in our direction. "He needs a fan."

"And a shower." Penelope rolled her eyes, taking a sip of the fruity cocktail she ordered for Naomi and me.

Having just finished my set for EverydayPPL, we decided to stop at a rooftop party at Elsie Rooftop to celebrate my biggest gig as a DJ. The pounding bass of an amapiano beat from the makeshift music booth reverberated as we settled into some VIP seating that Penelope had secured for us. The party was in full swing, with people mingling, dancing, and laughing like they had no worries in the world—saturated by the scents of sweat, sunscreen, over-priced perfume, and alcohol. Even as the sun began to set, the heat clung to the scene.

It was another beautiful New York summer, the kind that should've made anyone forget their troubles—at least temporarily.

"Onto other things... Cheers to Sol for a beautiful set and for getting another big DJ check!" Naomi raised her glass, and Penelope and I clinked our drinks against hers.

I took a sip of my drink. The flavors of passionfruit and rum dance on my tongue. "I still can't believe they reached out to me for it."

"I can!" Penelope continued, her sepia colored hands squeezing my shoulder. "You're picking up traction now that you're doing bigger gigs, so it only makes sense."

"First, it was Black House Radio performances," Naomi listed as she sipped her drink, "then Soulection Radio, now EverydayPPL—"

"Don't forget her Boiler Room gig that's happening in London next month," Penelope added.

"I haven't," Naomi nodded, continuing. "I just wanna know

if we can even afford to be her friends anymore since she's making it big time."

"Oh, please! I don't think the celebrity aesthetician has a right to make that comment," our friend Elizabeth said as she took a seat by us, looking at Naomi. "Last time I checked, you were busy doing people's faces for the Met Gala."

Her tawny finger pushed Naomi's oversized sunglasses up the bridge of her nose. Then, taking a seat between Naomi and me, Elizabeth chuckled.

"The shade." Naomi playfully swatted her arm before turning back to me. "But seriously, Sol, we're so proud of you. You killed it out there once again."

"I tried my best." I smiled gratefully at my friends, a warmth blooming in my chest at their words of encouragement.

"You didn't just try your best," Elizabeth said as she embraced me. "You killed that shit and everyone's been talking about it like they always do. Shiiiit... it makes me proud that you stepped out of your comfort zone to explore this DJ-ing full time."

DJ-ing was something I never imagined I'd have the courage to pursue full time—with my original day job as a game designer and all. I had gotten comfortable keeping it as a hobby—despite my love for music, posting videos here and there online and playing at small events for fun. However, thanks to a crappy relationship ending and the need for a new creative outlet that wasn't in the corporate world, the realization for some change in my life was needed.

And music came to the rescue.

The feeling of control over a crowd as they danced and vibed to the music mixed was intoxicating, addicting—like I was riding a high that I never wanted to come down from.

"Yeah, I still can't believe it myself." I sipped on my drink, relaxing further into the seat as I watched the party unfold... only to see a familiar face in the crowd.

Great.

Feeling a hand on my shoulder, I turned to see Penelope with her eyes squinting at me.

"You okay, girl?" she asked, her voice cutting through a mix of This Is How We Celebrate and Bhebha blasting through the speakers.

I forced a smile. "I'm good. Just... enjoying the view."

Her brows furrowed as she looked over to where I was gazing. She sighed upon seeing my ex-boyfriend lip-locked with some dark-skinned brunette I vaguely recognized from junior high—the same girl he once insisted was *just a friend*. The sight was like a sucker punch to my gut, knocking the wind out of me even though I knew it was coming.

It was hard to avoid him living in the same city; he had his friends and places he liked to frequent, and they always seemed to collide with my friends'.

"Seriously?" Naomi exclaimed, her light brown eyes widening in disbelief as she followed Penelope's gaze. "Is that asshole seriously here? Out of all places?"

"I thought this was an event solely for well-known creatives," Elizabeth said, tucking a strand of her brown curls behind her ear. "So how in the hell did his finance bro ass get in?"

I shrugged nonchalantly, trying to play it off like it was no big deal, but the sight of him stung more than I cared to admit.

How can he move on so quickly after... Well, everything?

Naomi leaned in closer, pushing aside the Senegalese twists that shielded her face. "Can I go be petty?"

I shook my head, trying to push down the surge of emotions threatening to rise up. "It's been nine months and I shouldn't be caring. Let him have his fun."

"And you guys were together for eight years." Penelope squeezed my hand gently. "You're allowed to feel a way about it, Sol. Y'all were just talking about finally considering couples therapy last month, and then he ghosted you. Now he's trying to move on to the next one, as if it's nothing. It's messed up."

"I know, but—" I cut myself off, the lump forming in my

throat making it hard to speak. My heart hammered in my chest as I watched him let the woman he was with grind against him without a care in the world.

"I hate that I still feel something for him," I admitted, my voice drowned out by the music. "It's been nine months since we've broken up, but every time I get over it, he slips in and tries to undo the work I've done."

Elizabeth wrapped an arm around my shoulders, pulling me in for a comforting side hug. "It's okay to still have feelings, Sol. Healing isn't a linear process."

"Well, it should be." I sighed. "I want to move on. I want to try dating for the first time in my life, especially since he was my first. I want something new for myself. Not constant reminders of him."

"You know what..." Naomi said, an evil smirk appearing across her face as she flicked her red coffin acrylics against the rim of her drink. "Just say the word. I haven't acted out in a week, and I'm down to stir the petty pot."

I chuckled at Naomi's offer, the corners of my lips curling up slightly despite the heaviness in my heart. "He's not worth it and never was. Besides, we're here to have a good time. Don't let him ruin it."

Naomi nodded, a mischievous glint in her brown eyes that made me slightly nervous as she chugged her cocktail, her gaze flickering back to my ex-boyfriend. "Okay, but..."

"But?" I glared.

She bit her lip. "I'm in the mood to dance and cause some chaos."

"Naomi." Penelope glared at her. "You better not—"

Too late.

Dusting off her cheetah tube dress, Naomi sprang to her feet, her Senegalese twists bouncing with each sway of her hips as she danced towards the makeshift dance floor.

"Oh lord..." I watched in mock horror as she slid her way between my ex and his new fling, breaking apart their intimate moment. The shock on my ex's face was priceless, quickly morphing into recognition, then annoyance, as Naomi continued to gyrate provocatively around them with another man, without missing a beat. Penelope buried her face in her hands as she murmured something about not being responsible for her actions, while Elizabeth burst into a fit of giggles.

"I can't believe this." I joined in on the laughter as my friend continued to annoy my ex.

"I—You know what?" Penelope threw her hands in the air, standing up as well. "Might as well have fun with her before shit hits the fan and she does something that gets us kicked out."

Elizabeth shook her head, laughing, accepting Penelope's extended hand and rose gracefully to her feet.

"You coming?" she turned to me, and I smiled at her, shaking my head *no.*

"I'm good." I gathered my swirl-printed silk long dress so I wouldn't accidentally trip over it while standing up. Throwing my empty cup into a nearby trash, I turned back to my friends. "I'm gonna go to the bar for another drink."

"And then you better join us," Penelope teased, flashing her dimpled smile as she pulled Elizabeth to the dance floor.

"Maybe!" I yelled after them, my voice lost in the thumping music. As I made my way towards the bar, I couldn't help but steal a glance back at my ex and his new fling, trying to pretend like nothing had happened—the smiles on their faces strained and forced. A pang of satisfaction fluttered in my chest at the sight of them feeling a fraction of the discomfort I had experienced moments before.

But as quickly as it came, it dissipated, leaving behind a hollowness that reminded me of the heartache still lingering. Seeing him move on with someone new after the way *he* took our break-up stirred negative emotions inside of me, threatening to drag me back into a place I had healed from.

It was unfair that my emotions were still at his mercy even after all this time.

However, I refuse to let his lying ass ruin the great day I had.

Today was about me performing an amazing set that had the crowd of EverydayPPL screaming for more. It was about doing something I never thought I'd be able to do.

It was about *my* win.

Not about him moving on with some rebound like he wasn't on my line a month ago—boohoo crying, asking me to give him another chance so we can rekindle whatever I thought we had.

But for once... *Just once*... I wanted his hold on me to vanish.

I was ready for something different.

New.

Sighing, I pushed through the crowd of people and finally reached the bar, the cool marble beneath my fingertips offering a slight reprieve from the warmth of the pulsating atmosphere. I leaned against the counter, catching the eye of the brown-skinned bartender who was busy mixing drinks amidst the sea of people shouting out drink orders over the current DJ's set.

"Can I get a mojito, please?" I said once I caught the attention of one of the bartenders.

"Actually," a deep male voice cut from behind me, sending a shiver down my spine. In my peripheral vision, a muscular hand extended a card to the bartender. "Make that two. One for the pretty lady, and one for me."

2 / SOLÈNE

He was tall.

Like I had to look up to see his face, tall.

With a muscular-lean build that I could tell came from a man with a proper gym discipline, his skin was a rich shade of golden oak, accentuated by the large rooftop lights that kissed it. His curly hair, a beautiful shade of ebony, was styled into a small fro that looked *too* perfect. He wore a simple black shirt and dark blue jeans that hugged his frame just right, leaving just enough to the imagination. His neck was adorned with a gold Cuban link and a second gold chain with a small pendant of the Dominican Republic bar coin.

"Thank you," he took his card back from the bartender and smiled, flashing me a view of diamond bottom bar grills on some of his perfectly straight, white teeth.

Damn, this man was high levels of fine.

Words stuck in my throat, I could only stare back at him while my heartbeat drummed in my ears. My palms felt clammy, my cheeks heated, and my mind went blank once when his eyes caught mine. They were deep, dark brown pools with flecks of gold that I wanted to drown in.

His smile widened, causing a dimple to appear in his left cheek.

"Your drink," he said, and my ears picked up the deep timbre of his voice... smooth and honeyed, like a sip of the finest whiskey. "It's behind you."

Bobbing my head as if it were loose, I reached for the mojito, unable to break eye contact. My hand clumsily hit the rim of the clear plastic cup, causing some of it to spill over my fingers.

"Shit." I gasped at the sensation of the cold liquid running down my hand. Reaching for a napkin, our hands connected as his reflexes were quick, catching mine in his.

"Let me help with that—"

"It's okay—" I shook my hand, wanting to retreat, but he held on, his touch sending my senses into overdrive. His eyes bore into mine, and I melted even more under his gaze.

"I want to." He brought my hand closer to him as he reached for a napkin. With a gentle motion, he dabbed at the spilled drink on my fingers, his touch feather-light and careful. Each contact gave me a flurry of butterflies in my stomach, and I unintentionally held my breath. As he cleaned with unwavering focus, I couldn't help but notice the intricate details of his hands—strong fingers, multiple rings, his nails meticulously trimmed and clean, and the contrast of his tanned skin against my umber hues.

When he finally looked up, our eyes locked once more, and I almost melted.

"Sorry about that," he continued.

I shook my head, attempting not to make a fool out of myself by squeaking. "No, it's... It's fine. T-thank you for helping. And thanks for the drink."

"Anytime." He flashed me another of those heart-stopping smiles before releasing my hand. "I don't mind paying for a drink for a beautiful woman."

I smiled nervously, blushing furiously at his compliment. "Well.. Thank you—"

"The name's Desiderio, but call me Desi."

"Desi." I nodded, feeling a rush of warmth spread through me at the sound of his name. "Sounds Latin."

"It is," he nodded. "Born in the DR, raised in the Bronx."

"I could tell by your necklace."

He chuckled, his fingers touching the bar coin pendant. "What about you?"

"I'm from D.C, but my family moved to Brooklyn freshman year of high school."

"BK? Makes sense." A smirk appeared on his face.

I pursed my lips as my eyes turned to slits. "What?"

"Brooklyn always has gorgeous women." He winked and I blushed. "Where in Brooklyn?"

"Fort Greene. I grew up around the big park. Lived right off of Clermont until I moved to Williamsburg. You?"

"I was raised in Parkchester until my family moved to Riverdale. Oh, that reminds me... I never caught your name."

"Sorry about that. I'm–"

"Girl! We been looking everywhere for you and—oh!" Naomi grasped my shoulder, her eyes widening as she took in the scene before her. I cleared my throat, tearing my gaze away from Desi to awkwardly smile at my best friend as if I'd been caught doing something I wasn't supposed to do.

"Naomi, this is Desi." I gestured towards the man standing beside me. "He... uhm.. he was just helping me with... I spilled my drink."

"Nice to meet you, Naomi." He extended a hand to shake hers, which she took with a grin.

"Likewise." Shifting her attention between Desiderio and me, a smirk appeared on her lips before she turned to me.

"What's up?" I looked at her, my cheeks feeling warmer under her knowing gaze, and it caused her smirk to grow.

"Nell and I was looking for you to come dance with us but..." She paused as she eyed Desi again, and then turned to me and winked. "I'll let her and Liz know you're all good."

"I was just grabbing a drink. I can come now—"

She held her hand up. "Naaaaah. Have fun here with *Desi*."

She turned back to him with a sly grin. “Make sure she doesn’t spill any more drinks, sir. Can you promise me that?”

“I’ll try.” He nodded with a chuckle, and I did my best to ignore the flutter in my heart at the sound. Shooting me one last mischievous smile followed by a wink, Naomi disappeared into the crowd, leaving me alone with Desiderio, who was still wearing that disarming grin.

“Looks like I’ve been assigned as your drink spillage prevention specialist,” he joked.

I let out a nervous laugh, biting my lip. “Well, I promise I’m not usually this clumsy.”

“Oh really?” He raised an eyebrow, his expression playful. “Had me fooled for a second there.”

I rolled my eyes at his teasing, but couldn't suppress the smile that tugged at my lips.

“You have a nice smile,” he continued, taking a sip of his drink. “Don’t try to hide it.”

“I—” I felt myself turn into a tomato at his compliment. “T-thank you.”

“Mhm.” He leaned casually against the bar counter, his eyes never leaving mine. “So, spill-prone, what brings—”

I gasped, holding my hand to my chest in mock offense. “Spill-prone?”

“You never told me your name,” he quipped, taking another sip of his drink. “It’s gonna be *spill-prone* until you tell me your name.”

“It’s Solène.”

“*Solène.*” He gave me a nod, rolling my name around on his tongue as if testing it. “French?”

“Mhm.” I nodded, finally taking a sip of my drink. “Haitian grandparents.”

“Interesting.” He mused with a slight tilt of his head, as if intrigued by this new piece of information while silence settled between us, the music and chatter from the surrounding crowd filling the gap.

"So, Solène with the spill-prone tendencies," Desi finally broke the silence. "What brings you out here tonight?"

I sucked my teeth, pretending to be offended. "You're not gonna let go of the spill-prone nickname, are you?"

"Nah." He grinned, his dimple making another appearance. "It's either that or I can call you Butterfingers."

"Butterfingers?" I wrinkled my nose at the suggestion, playfully swatting his arm. "C'mon, now you're just being mean."

"Butterfingers, spill-prone Solène—" he started, but I cut him off with a playful glare, making him laugh even more. "Okay, okay, I'll stop." He raised his hands in surrender, still grinning from ear to ear.

"I think you can come up with a better nickname for me, or even better... just call me Sol."

He chuckled, tapping his chin. "Sol like the sun? It works, considering that you've brightened my evening."

I tilted my head. "Are you always this smooth, Desi?"

"Maybe." He smirked, leaning in a little closer. His scent, a mixture of sandalwood, mint and something distinctly him enveloped me. "Only when I meet someone worth the effort."

This man's too charming.

I laughed. "Such a cornball."

"A corn-ball that got you blushing and giggling," he pointed out, which earned him another giggle. "So, back to my question, Spill-prone. What brings you here tonight?"

3 / DESIDERIO

SOLÈNE WAS...

Mierda, words can't describe how fine this woman is.

Skin a gorgeous color of mahogany, I fell into a trance the minute I saw her walk in with that long dress that hugged all the right places. Don't fault me for looking, but I couldn't tear my eyes away.

New York was filled with beautiful Black women, so it wasn't a surprise to stumble upon one every now and then. However, Solène was different, intriguing me to admire from afar and keep pushing.

I'm leaving soon anyways so might as well enjoy the view 'till I can't.

Exhausted from a long day at work, I wasn't interested in engaging in flirtatious—or any other types of interactions. My goal was to support my best friend's event, as I had made a promise to show up, greet a couple of people, and then take my Black ass home.

But once I watched her long terracotta curls sway as she headed to the bar by herself? Suddenly, the decision to leave felt premature. I found myself inching closer, wanting more.

Next thing you know?

I'm walking over, buying her a drink and striking up a conversation despite my heart racing a million miles a minute 'cause everything about her was... whew.

"So, back to my question, Sol," I said, my eyes dancing over her features for the hundredth time. "What brings you here tonight?"

Sipping on her mojito, her large brown eyes peered up at me, and I found myself getting lost in them.

"My friends brought me here." Her eyes left mine, looking into the crowd of people dancing as if searching for someone, before they returned to me. "We just came from EverydayPPL, and Naomi told us about the invite she got for an event at Elsie. What about you?"

"Just here to support my friend's event before I head home."

"Wait." Her brows furrowed. "Your friend's event... Is Tony—as in the host—your friend?"

I nodded. "We go way back. You know him?"

"Naomi does." She gave me one of her giggles that had me grinning like a little kid internally every time I heard it. "I mean... I met him a couple of times in college when she brought him around, but I don't know him like that. He a cool dude though."

"Well shit. New York's really a small world," I mused. "Everyone's always connected in some way."

"Tell me about it." She took another sip of her mojito, her eyes lingering on mine, then my lips for a beat too long before she looked away.

Silence took over the air between us, and I kept my eyes on her, trying to figure out how to keep the conversation going. Though it was brief, shit between us flowed effortlessly like we had known each other for a while, and I wasn't ready to let her slip away just yet.

After what felt like minutes but was probably only seconds of us standing here, a new DJ appeared at the booth and switched up the tempo, starting his set with 4 Kampé II, and I couldn't believe my luck. Without a second thought, I set my drink down.

"Spill-prone, you in the mood to dance?" I asked, praying she wouldn't turn me down.

She giggled. "We're back to spill-prone?"

"I'm just messing." I winked, holding out my hand to her. "But seriously though, you wanna dance?"

She bit those plump lips of hers, covered by a gloss. "Uhm..."

"You don't have to accept if you don't want to." Although I wish she would.

The idea of her in my arms while we danced—giving me the opportunity to take in the way her body moved—had me on edge. Just looking at her was a visual feast, but the thought of actually holding her close, being able to let the vanilla and coconut fragrance that wafted off her skin, intoxicate me further?

That would put me through the wringer, but I didn't care.

She took another look at the crowd and then back at me, slipping her hand into mine. "Don't expect me to be some kompa queen just 'cause I said I had Haitian in me."

"I ain't asking you to be." My thumb grazed over her knuckles once it was in my grasp. "I wanna vibe with you a little longer."

Leading her onto the dance floor, we found a spot in the midst of swirling bodies and began moving to the beat. One hand on her waist with the other on her back, our steps naturally aligned like two puzzle pieces perfectly designed to fit together. Every sway was as if we were one, every step like a conversation in itself; a language only we understood.

"I thought you didn't know how to dance." I moved my hands lower on her waist to pull her closer, rocking my hips in sync with hers.

"I never said that." She laughed, looking into my eyes as if she were hypnotizing me. "I just said I wasn't a pro."

"You feel like a pro to me," I whispered before drawing her closer until there was barely any space left between us.

As we continued dancing, I used the opportunity of our closeness to appreciate her beauty up close. Her curls, styled into a half-up, half-down braided hairstyle, bounced and swayed with every movement of her hips. Her amber eyes sparkled each time the light hit them, and her fingernails grazing the back of my neck —it felt like a dream.

It was as if we were the only two people in the room, and I never wanted it to end.

So when the song finally ended, we stood there for a moment, our bodies still close, our breathing in sync, and continued dancing to the next set of slow songs without missing a beat. Even though the crowd around grew smaller and the party seemed to thin out, it didn't matter to me.

I didn't want this night to end, not when being with her felt like the most natural thing in the world.

Once the fifth song lulled, and the crowd was barely there to give us a quiet moment....

I did the one thing that went against what I had originally planned this evening.

I paused and looked down at the beauty, whispering close to her ear, "Do you wanna spend more time with me tonight?"

4 / SOLÈNE

[Naomi:] Have y'all fucked yet? How's he in bed? 😈

[Me:] 😑 really Mimi? I just met the guy.

[Lizzy:] Naomi Browne-Amoros!

[Naomi:] What?? One night stands aren't bad!

[Nell:] Let the girl enjoy her damn date!

[Nell:] jfc Mimi… 🙄

[Naomi:] I'm asking the right questions!!!! Y'all need to stop acting like u don't wanna know too!The man's fine! She better hit!

[Allie:] Wait… Sol… you on a date?? With who??

[Me:] Not really…

[Lizzy:] Yup! She met a cute guy at T's party and agreed to go out with him when he asked her out.

[Allie:] I always miss out cause of work! Dammit! 😠

[Naomi:] Should've been there, Allie. U would've enjoyed the show.

[Me:] It's not a date, Allie 🙃. I'm just hanging out with him.

[Nell:] Girl pls. 😒

[Naomi:] Hanging out, my ass. Let me know when y'all fucked yet.

[Naomi:] & girl, get off ur phone! Go enjoy your new man!

"EVERYTHING GOOD?" I heard Desiderio's voice, and I looked up from my phone to see him staring at me with a pinched face as he took a seat across from me, holding a brown paper bag.

After agreeing to spend the rest of the evening with him—since Naomi and Penelope insisted that I go, Desi and I decided to embark on whatever adventure he had planned. Though I was initially hesitant because I hardly knew him, nor had I done something like this before, the thought of spending more time with him wasn't entirely unwelcome.

He seemed harmless, and truth be told? I was curious about what he had in store for the night.

Once my friends and I confirmed that we were all aligned—Naomi was committed to ensuring my safety, Penelope vowed to extract me from any situation if I texted the chat our code word, Elizabeth was on top of location tracking, and Alexandra had her phone on standby for any last-minute saves—Desi and I headed to our first destination of the evening: Empanada Mama in East Village.

Quickly silencing my phone, I locked it and set it on the wooden tan table. "I'm good. My friends just checking in."

"You can let them know that you're fine and that I'm no serial killer." He smirked, passing me a bottled cherry lemonade—but not before opening it for me. "Although, maybe that's what a serial killer would say."

"Thank you." I took the drink from him with a laugh. "And good luck getting away with it. My friends don't play. They'll have your body in pieces all over the city before midnight."

He arched an eyebrow, leaning back into the turquoise seat. "I guess I'll be on my best behavior then."

"You don't have a choice." I stuck out my tongue at him. Grabbing my empanada, I took a bite of the warm pastry filled with braised oxtail, plantains, and carrots. As I chewed, enjoying the savory flavors, I noticed him watching me intently.

"What?" I narrowed my eyes at him, swallowing before taking another sip of my lemonade.

Desi's gaze lingered on me for a moment longer before he shook his head with a small smile. "Nothing."

"Do I have something on my face..." I started touching around my lips, feeling self-conscious all of a sudden. He chuckled softly and reached over, his thumb hovering over my cheek.

"May I?" his eyes searched mine for a *yes,* and I nodded, my heart fluttering in my chest as he gently brushed his thumb across my cheek to wipe away a stray crumb. His touch was surprisingly tender, causing me to hold my breath for a moment.

"There," he said softly, wiping away the dipping sauce that spilled. My brain was still processing the intimate gesture when he lifted his thumb to his lips, his gaze meeting mine.

Did he just... I blinked at him, caught off guard by the unexpected boldness of him licking his thumb clean. His eyes, still holding mine, were dark and intense, as if silently daring me to react. For a moment, time froze around us, and I felt a warmth pulsing between my legs.

Clearing my throat, I shifted in my seat.

"Flirt." I gave him a playful shove before taking a hurried sip of my cherry lemonade, needing something to cool down the sudden heat in my cheeks.

He ate the last bit of his viagra empanada—an empanada made with seafood. "I'm making sure you don't walk around with sauce on your face all night, Spill-prone." Leaning in closer, his voice dropping to a whisper. "Unless that's your thing, then," he licked his lips and winked. "I could always help you with that."

I nearly choked on my drink at his words, and he leaned back again in his seat, bursting out laughing.

"Let me stop." He raised his hands in mock surrender, and I threw a napkin at him, which he caught with a smug grin.

"You are something else." I shook my head, trying to suppress my own laughter as I continued eating.

He snickered, taking a sip of his mango juice. "I'm taking that as a good thing."

"Take it however you wanna take it, Mr. Flirt."

"Huh." He crossed his arms, wiggling his eyebrows. "Mr. Flirt? I kinda like it."

I playfully scoffed as I finished off my empanada, looking at him through lowered lashes.

This man was proving to be more captivating than I had anticipated, his easy charm and quick wit drawing me in without much effort.

After a moment of comfortable silence between us while we finished our meals, he cleared his throat and looked at me intently. "So, Butterfingers—"

Him and his nicknames. "You like getting me riled up, don't you?"

"I plead the fifth, buuuut..." He pouted, his voice turning teasing. "It's kind of fun to see your reactions..." I noticed a shift in his gaze then, something softer. "But if you don't seriously like them, then I can stop."

"Nah, it's fine. I mean, they're growing on me..." I trailed off, realizing how easily I admitted that. Desi's eyes sparkled as he leaned back in his seat, his smile widening.

"I knew it," He exclaimed triumphantly, making me laugh at his playfulness. "But hey, if you ever want me to stop, just say the word."

"Noted," I replied with a grin. "But you do realize that means you'll have to come up with new ones, right?"

"Oh, the challenge has been accepted, Butterfly," he said with a wink.

I couldn't help but roll my eyes at the new addition to his ever-growing list of pet names for me. "Butterfly now, huh?"

"Consider Butterfly an upgrade."

I let out a laugh, shaking my head in mock exasperation. "Lucky me."

"Well, in that case..." He rose from his seat and extended his hand towards me. "Shall we get going, my Butterfly?"

I placed my hand in his, feeling a tingle run up my arm at his touch. "Where are we going?"

"Don't worry," he said as he led me towards the exit after throwing away our trash and opening the door for me. "It's a surprise."

5 / DESIDERIO

"I HAVE A QUESTION," Solène said as we walked the block towards the L train entrance.

"Ask away."

"Other than my name and age... You haven't asked me anything else about myself."

"I have my reasons."

Looking down at her, I saw her expression shift to one of curiosity, so I decided to satisfy her unasked question.

"I haven't asked 'cause I learn people from their actions," I continued, maneuvering her out of the flow of nightly pedestrian traffic with a gentle hand on her back. "I observe and it tells me everything I need to know about a person."

"Like?"

Opening the subway glass entrance door for her to enter first once we arrived at the station, I kept my eyes fixed on her as she stepped through.

"Like the way you hesitated before stepping onto the escalator just now," I said as we descended underground towards the payment machines. "Tells me that you're cautious, maybe even a bit wary of new situations. It's also the reason why you went to your friends when I asked to spend more time with you. You needed some reassurance before you said yes."

She looked back at me with wide eyes as if I had revealed a big secret of hers.

“Am I wrong?”

“What else?” She ignored my question as we approached the turnstiles. I swiped my subway card and held the gate open for her to follow through.

"Another is how you refused to take an Uber—or a taxi—even though I offered to pay," I noted as we approached the platform and found a place to stand. "Tells me that you value your independence and prefer to rely on yourself rather than others for assistance.”

“Or it could be that I prefer the subway over trying to navigate traffic in a cramped car.”

I scrunched my mouth at her, not believing her lie. “You really want me to believe the subway system in New York City is more appealing than a comfortable car ride?”

She chuckled, shaking her head. “Believe what you want, but the subway got its own charm.”

“Other than the occasional performances and musicians, the random spoken word poetry, and the snack people? There’s nothing fun about a train that’s always either late, overcrowded or smells like piss. Don’t let me get started on the high school kids and rush hour.”

Just then, an announcement came through, letting everyone on the platform know that the train would be delayed by fifteen minutes.

I smirked. “Look at God proving my point.”

"Bruhhhh..." She grumbled, crossing her arms, which made her chest puff out in a way that I found distracting.

Yet I quickly shook off the thought and focused on the conversation at hand.

"Now we have more time for me to learn about you through your actions.”

“Yeah, yeah, yeah, anyways.” She shooed away my teasing with a wave of her hand. “You still never answered my question.”

"Which one?"

"Why didn't you ask me about myself?'

I got into her personal space, giving her no options but to look up at me.

"If I ask you everything so early." I leaned closer until our faces were only inches apart. "Then how can I spend more time with you? How can I show you how much I pay attention to the little details that make you who you are?"

Solène's breath hitched as she searched my eyes for an answer. I watched as her lips parted ever so slightly, her eyes flickering between my eyes and my lips.

"I guess you have a point."

"I do." I smiled, enjoying the effect my proximity had on her, as if it wasn't also affecting me in the same way. "I like taking my time with my treasure."

"Treasure?"

"Mhmm."

The dim lighting of the subway platform, casting shadows across her face, made her look even more alluring. She looked delectable, and it took all my self-control not to close the small gap between us and kiss her right then and there.

However, my mind intervened.

Is this going to be another casual thing, or... was this going to be more?

Are we only hanging out tonight and going with the flow until we part ways, or do I want more than that?

Do I care enough to get to know her past my observations? Everything about her beyond surface level shit?

What exactly was I looking for?

Before my thoughts could spiral any further, the loud screeching of the approaching train interrupted our moment.

"Well," I said, taking a step back to give her space, "looks like our chariot has arrived early."

As the train came to a stop in front of us, its doors slid open and we stepped inside an empty cart—save for another person sitting in the corner engrossed in a book. Solène found an empty seat by the window, and I sat down next to her.

"About those questions of yours," I began, turning to face her as the train started moving. "I think I got a few to ask."

6 / SOLÈNE

WE TALKED the entire subway ride.

Seated by one another, we shared details about our childhood, our work lives, and personal hobbies... even seemingly trivial details that we felt held no importance—yet made the conversation intimate.

Even when we had to switch from the L to the 5, we didn't miss a beat.

With each topic, I found myself opening up to him in a way that I hadn't done before with a stranger. His easy smile and genuine interest in what I had to say put me at ease, despite the nerves that had been fluttering in my stomach ever since we first met at Elsie's.

For once, I didn't feel the need to guard my heart or put up walls. Instead, I let myself just be vulnerable, letting the words flow freely without overthinking. It was strange how comfortable I felt with someone I had only just met, as if we had known each other for years. His presence was reassuring, and the way he listened, like really listened, made me feel heard in a way I didn't know I needed.

In just a small amount of time, he achieved something that took my ex months to do.

"So let me get this straight," he tried not to laugh, taking deep breaths to compose himself as my cheeks flushed in embarrassment. "You did what?"

I groaned and buried my face in my hands. "I thought my friends and I could fix the hole Nell's sister made in the ceiling by painting on top of it! I was not gonna get my ass whooped for her not knowing the difference between the soft part and the hard part."

"And this is why you don't let seven-year-olds play hide and seek in the attic," he took another deep breath, which resulted in him throwing his head back and laughing. I couldn't help but join in.

"Okay, Mr. Art Director," I groaned again, still laughing. "You can chill out now. Not everyone can be as artistic as you."

"Just know that the next time I need a paint job done on set," he said in between fits of laughter. "I'll call you."

I playfully elbowed him. "I'll have you know my painting skills improved since then."

"I'll be the judge of it," he said, still chuckling under his breath."Gotta see it with my own eyes first."

"I swear. I've gotten better and even painted my—" I paused, the memory of my ex flooding my mind, threatening to overshadow the warm moment Desi and I were having. Taking a deep breath, I pushed the unwelcome memories aside and smiled. "Enough about me, tell me about yourself."

"Sensitive territory?"

My brows furrowed.

"If I summoned up something too painful to talk about, I apologize."

"No, it's not that. It's just—" I shifted uncomfortably in my seat, biting my lip. My fingers began to play with the fabric of my dress as the train made another stop and the door slid open, letting out the only person who occupied the cart with us.

I took a moment to compose myself before meeting his gaze. "The last person whose place I painted—well, helped paint his room—was my ex."

"Oh... I see how that could be a touchy subject. I ain't mean to—"

"He was bound to be brought up in conversation tonight, so I shrugged, a smile tugging at the corners of my lips. "Might as well rip off the band-aid now, right?"

He took my hand into his, his thumb gently rubbing circles on the back of my hand. "You don't have to if you don't want to."

"I don't mind."

"Are you sure?"

I didn't know, but something in me trusted him enough to share.

"I'm sure," I nodded, releasing a slow breath as the stress in my shoulders gradually dissolved with each motion.

"He was... I guess you could say he was my high school sweetheart. My first everything. Dated senior year, then we broke up second year of college and then got back together again, only for the pattern to repeat."

He gently squeezed my hand as if to offer comfort in his touch.

"Things were... complicated, to say the least," I continued. "We—well, I thought we could make it work, but in the end, it just wasn't meant to be. Too many differences, too many expectations. Too many times, he was caught up in his own world, leaving me to fend for myself. I was always trying to fit into his life, his plans, his dreams, and I lost sight of what I wanted along the way. Eventually, it all fell apart. Now, at twenty-six years old, I realize that my happiness shouldn't be dependent on someone else... That I accepted for less because... he was my first... love."

"Woah..."

Letting out a bitter chuckle, I blinked away the tears that wanted to fall. "It's funny how you think you know what love is supposed to feel like at such a young age because the movies always make it seem so easy, only to realize years later that maybe it was just infatuation masquerading as something more profound. But... Hey, enough about my tragic love story. I don't want to bore you with my drama on our first meeting."

"You're not boring me at all."

Using his thumb, he brought my face to look up at his.

"You could never bore me with anything you gotta tell me," he whispered, his eyes searching mine with a depth that made my heart skip a beat. "I want to know everything about you, the good and the bad. It's what makes you who you are, and I want to understand you better."

His thumb caressing my cheek felt like a gentle breeze; it soothed and calmed me in a way I hadn't expected.

Making me realize that I was... I was falling for him after one night's hang-out.

Fuck.

That was terrifying.

It'd been so long since I felt butterflies or my heart race, and yet here he was, stirring up emotions that I thought would take forever to resurface because of how deeply it was buried.

I swallowed hard.

This felt too soon, too fast, but with him...

"If anything," he murmured, interrupting my train of thought. "You sharing your beautiful story with me makes me feel like I'm lacking in the love department."

"How?"

"You shared something personal, so I should do the same to level the playing field, right?" He chuckled, his gaze holding mine captive. "Well, get ready for this heartbreaker: I'm twenty-eight and I've never been in a serious relationship. Never experienced a heartbreak before."

His revelation caught me off guard.

A man like him, charming and kind-hearted, had never been in a serious relationship?

Now it made sense why he seemed so unaffected by the weight of emotional baggage; he was carrying an empty suitcase.

"It's not that I haven't tried or wanted to," he confessed,

pulling his hand away from my face to rub his neck, and my mind cursed my sudden eagerness to feel his touch once more. "But it just never seemed to work out. I've dated here and there, tried pursuing something serious in college... But nothing ever clicked enough to pursue something long-term. It's hard to explain, but everything was... casual."

"Love has a funny way of sneaking up on you when you least expect it." I reached out to lightly squeeze his hand. "Maybe you just haven't met the right person yet."

"Or maybe the universe was telling me I wasn't ready."

"Well.. Are you ready now?"

He nodded, his gaze softening as he looked at me.

"Absolutely," he whispered, his voice barely above a breath. "I been ready."

I felt a sudden heat take over my body as his words registered within me. Maintaining eye contact, I found myself lost in the depth of his gaze, feeling a connection forming between us that was undeniable. It was as if the universe had conspired to bring us together tonight, igniting a spark that neither of us could ignore.

Without breaking the intense eye contact, he slowly closed the gap between us, his hand reaching back up to gently brush a stray strand of hair away from my face. The touch sent shivers down my spine, awakening a dormant need within me that I had long forgotten. In that brief moment of contact, a rush of emotions floods through me—longing, desire, and a flicker of something dangerously close to infatuation.

As his thumb traced a soft caress along my cheek, I found myself leaning into his touch, craving the warmth and comfort he offered. The world around us seemed to fade into the background, nothing but the two of us existing in our own bubble.

He leaned in closer, his lips hovering just inches away from mine.

"You're so beautiful," he breathed, and every nerve in my body became on high alert, every fiber of my being yearning to bridge the gap that remained.

And so I closed my eyes, allowing myself to lean in the rest of the way.... only for the train to come to a halt, the announcement of Pelham Pkwy echoing through the car, jolting us back to reality. We both froze, our faces mere centimeters apart.

Slowly, he pulled back his hand, dropping from my cheek as he stood to his feet.

"We're here," he extended his hand for me to take. "Time for you to see your surprise."

7 / DESIDERIO

“So...” she said as we walked down White Plains Road, her hand in mine so she wouldn’t trip on the concrete pavement. “What’s this surprise?”

“It wouldn’t be a surprise if I told you.”

“Buuut,” she dragged out the word, her voice teasing and sweet like the syrup from the corner diner. "If you told me, I could act surprised.”

I glanced down at her, the golden light of the streetlamp casting a soft glow over her face, making her red hair appear deeper and her skin almost luminous.

"Acting surprised doesn't count. I’m not telling you anything. You’ll have to wait."

Her pout deepened, making me suppress a grin.

Though it was inching one in the morning, the streets of Pelham Parkway, a neighborhood in the Bronx, were still somewhat alive. Sounds of distant car horns and muffled reggaeton from bars filled the air. There was a barbecue happening outside an apartment complex, where a couple of people laughed and drank, and someone was playing the saxophone at the end of the block, where a bodega was still open.

Rounding the corner on Lydig Ave, I steered her towards a home nestled between old brick buildings, and we stopped.

"Are we here?" She looked up at me, her eyes shining like a kid on Christmas morning. She looked around for a sign and found none. "What is this place?"

"Close your eyes and you'll find out."

"You're not gonna kill me, are you?"

I laughed, shaking my head. "Nah, nothing like that. Trust me."

"If you try," her eyes narrowed, trying to keep a serious face on, however, the smile creeping in worked against her. "My friends—"

"Will have my body chopped up, floating in the Hudson, I know," I finished for her. "I ain't gonna do you like that."

Biting her lip, she hesitated for a moment before complying. "Okay, they're closed."

Double-checking they were closed, I placed my hands onto her ears and led her up the steps of the stoop, pushing open the home's brown door. Greeting the old Black man at the wooden counter with a codeword—along with the bouncer who held the secret entrance open for me, I walked her through a door disguised as a bookshelf and down a set of stairs until we reached the hidden space: an underground jazz speakeasy.

Placing myself behind her, I removed my hands from her ears as I whispered."Okay, you can open them now."

The room was lit with red candlelights, casting soft shadows on exposed brick walls. The air was thick with the smell of cigar smoke and whiskey, mixed with the sound of Latin jazz music drifting from a live Afro-Cuban band in the corner. On one side was a wood, dark red bar, and on the other were vinyls dated all the way to the fifties.

"Oh my god," she gasped, her hand flying up to cover her mouth in shock once she took her fill of the space.

"You like?'

She turned around to me, beaming. "I'm in love!"

Taking her hand in mine, I led her towards a small booth closer to where the band was. As we settled into our seats, she couldn't contain her excitement, her eyes darting around the speakeasy, taking in every detail.

"How'd you find out about this place?"

"My parents love jazz music and played it all the time, so I fell in love with it too," I explained, flagging down the bartender for some drinks. "Found this place a couple of years ago thanks to the owner briefly being our neighbor."

"This place is so cool," she continued, looking around until her eyes found mine. "Thank you for bringing me here. This is an amazing surprise."

"Happy to know you like it."

"Correction: I love the place."

"Let me correct myself," I held my hands up in mock surrender, amused. "Happy to know you *love* it."

"Thank you," she stuck out her tongue at me, a ghost of a smile on her lips. "Get it right."

"Yeah, yeah, yeah," I rolled my eyes, sliding her the specialty purple pink cocktail in a couple glass the male bartender set down for us. "Here. Taste."

"So demanding," she took the drink from me, her fingers lingered on mine, creating a friction that sent my pulse in overdrive. I watched as she brought the glass to her slightly parted lips, her eyes never leaving mine as she took a sip. Her reaction was instant—a slow smile crept across her face, followed by a little hum of approval as she set it back down.

"Okay," she said, leaning in closer so her voice wouldn't be lost in the music. "This is fire. What is it?"

I smirked, leaning back in my seat and letting my arm drape lazily over the backrest of the booth. "They call it *La Melodia*—after a Latin jazz song. One of their signature cocktails with grenadine, raspberry, and blueberries. I'm guessing you love it?"

"I think..." she paused, swirling the drink in her glass, pretending to deliberate as her lips curled into a wicked grin, "I'll need another before I decide."

"Another? Really, Butterfingers?"

She laughed, yet this time… it felt different. It was like it was meant for me.

"Back to slandering me now?"

"I'm just saying," I teased, tilting my head with a mock-stern expression, "I was there when you almost spilled all of your mojito. What's to say you won't spill this one too?"

She laughed again, and I felt my chest tighten in a way that threw me off guard.

Whew.

Was I… falling for her?

The thought struck me like a lightning bolt, sudden and impossible to ignore. My teasing grin faltered for a moment, but I recovered quickly, masking the rush of emotions with a chuckle of my own.

Did… was I seriously catching feelings?

Actually… I *already* caught feelings, didn't I?

8 / DESIDERIO

I WAS STILL unsure of what I wanted, however, I knew how I felt.

Like I had told myself earlier, my original plan was only to admire her and keep it pushing.

I wasn't interested in entertaining anything romantic—not because I was scared or unready, but because I wasn't sure what would blossom out of our interaction. Used to flings that never made it past the preliminary stage, I had grown comfortable with the fleeting nature of connections.

They came, they went, and they left no more than an echo.

Yet as we spent more time together... something started to shift.

And it made me want to dive deeper into who she was, craving to further understand her.

However, I had to ask myself if it was just the allure of something new, something unexplored, that was pulling me in...

Or was it something real?

I had to ask myself what I wanted with this beautiful woman who I just met a couple of hours ago.

What was my next plan?

Where did I go from here?

I didn't have the answer to these things, however, I knew one thing: I caught feelings and I wasn't sure how to handle them.

"Alright," she said, setting down her glass with a satisfied clink. "I've decided."

"Have you now?" I asked, fighting to keep my tone light despite the internal chaos.

Ay mami.

When did it get so damn hard to breathe?

She nodded, raising an eyebrow like she was about to present me with the most important thing known to man.

"This drink? Absolute ten out of ten." She gestured dramatically toward the glass. "In fact, it might be my new favorite thing."

My lips twitched into a grin as I leaned in closer, resting my forearm on the table between us. "Your new favorite thing, huh? That's a bold statement. You sure about that, Spill-Prone?"

"Absolutely sure. You're tripping if you try to tell me they got something better than this... wait, do they?"

I nodded, though I wasn't really sure what I was agreeing to.

My focus had narrowed entirely on her—a lockdown of my senses I hadn't prepared for.

The way she talked was full of energy—her hands emphasized every word, and her head tilted slightly when she laughed. It all appeared so natural, as if she was entirely free from any self-consciousness.

Why was I picking up on these things so much?

Each tilt of her head, each flick of her fingers, each easy grin—none of it should have mattered, yet all of it did. I was being overly observant... maybe even *ridiculous* because I was cataloguing things that made no sense to keep track of.

"So what about you?" she asked suddenly, shifting the spotlight back onto me as she rested her chin in her palm.

I cleared my throat, suddenly feeling like a deer caught in headlights. "What about me?"

"You know more about me than I know about you," she said, licking her lip, and the sight of her undid me. Her tongue darted out just for a second, and the gesture was enough to derail my train of thought, imagining inappropriate things I had no business thinking about.

"You know about my obsession with this drink," she continued, oblivious to the spiral my mind had just taken. "You know what I do for a living, my obsession with old school songs and indie films, that I love pilates and ballet, *and* how I apparently have a habit of spilling things, which, for the record, I don't think is entirely fair. But what about you? What's something I should know?"

"You know enough about me—"

"I know about your love life, that you're the oldest of three with two younger sisters, you're an art director who loves to observe people, you like cooking because your abuela taught you, the fact that you're a Dominican from the Bronx—but that's obvious—"

I fake-gasped. "That's obvious?"

"Sir," she smacked her lips and rolled those beautiful eyes of hers. "You have a DR chain on. It's obvious that you're a papi—omg did I just say something cringe out loud?"

I laughed, shaking my head. "Papi? That's how you see me? That's my new nickname?"

"I never meant—" she paused, catching onto my deflecting and narrowing her eyes at me like she was figuring out a puzzle. "You're slick. I see what you're doing."

I batted my eyelashes. "Doing what?"

"You're not getting off that easy."

"But you got me all figured out. You even got a nickname for me now."

"Barely," she shot back. "Barely is the key word here. I've only scratched the surface, but I want more."

"Then ask for more," my voice lowered an octave as I leaned forward into her personal space, and she didn't back away. Instead, she held her ground, her gaze steady, though I noticed the faintest rise in her chest as she inhaled.

"What's something you've never told anyone?" Her voice was suddenly softer, filled with a sexual undertone, and it turned me on in a way that made my pulse quicken. I swallowed hard, trying to steady myself, yet her proximity was wrecking my composure.

"A secret?" My voice came out a lot deeper and breathier than I intended, betraying exactly how much she affected me.

"Yes," she replied, leaning in just a fraction closer, as if daring me to close the gap entirely.

Ay... *Dios, ayúdame.*

I ran my thumb along the edge of my glass, stalling as I dug through myself for something small enough to offer yet big enough to mean something. Finally, I stopped fidgeting and looked at her dead-on.

"I'm terrified of losing control."

Her eyes softened at my confession, and for a moment, she didn't say anything—just studied me like she was trying to see past it all. Past the guarded layers, past the smooth deflections. My heart pounded in my chest, each beat echoing in my ears as I waited for her reaction.

"Control," she repeated quietly, almost to herself. She leaned back slightly, however, her gaze never wavered from mine. "Like what kind of control?"

I shrugged and forced a small chuckle, trying to lighten the moment even though it felt like I had just exposed a nerve. "The kind that keeps everything in check. Keeps people at a distance or situations from getting... messy."

Her lips curved into a faint, knowing smile. "Messy like spilled drinks?"

"No, Spill-prone," I chuckled, shaking my head. "Messy like emotions."

She tilted her head, considering that for a moment. Her fingers absentmindedly traced patterns on the table between us.

"That's heavy... You do realize that it's a human thing to be a little messy, right?"

I grimaced. "Yeah, I get that. But it doesn't mean I like it."

She studied me for a moment, her expression unreadable, then leaned forward again, closing the distance I hadn't realized had grown between us. Her hair caught the low light of the bar, shimmering like some kind of halo, and suddenly, I wasn't sure if my confession had made her more intrigued or if she was quietly plotting my demise with all this closeness.

"Maybe you don't have to like it," she said finally, her voice a low murmur that tangled itself around me, pulling me deeper into her magnetic pull. "Maybe you just have to accept it. Let it... happen for once and you'll see that it's not so bad."

I opened my mouth to respond—to deflect or make a joke or something that would put me back on solid ground—yet nothing came out.

She disarming me with just a few words.

Smirking at my silence, it was almost as if she knew exactly what was happening inside my head. That infuriatingly beautiful smirk—it was the kind of expression that made you want to both kiss someone senseless and argue with them just for the sake of seeing what else might unfold.

I leaned back slightly, trying to regain some sense of control, but her gaze followed me like it was tethered to mine.

"You make it sound so easy."

"Who said it's supposed to be easy?" she shrugged, her hand moving to cradle her empty glass, swirling the liquid inside absently. "The good things never are."

"Is that your philosophy on life?" I asked, raising an eyebrow.

"Maybe," she said. "Do you disagree?"

"I—" I paused. "I don't know if I agree or disagree with you yet."

"Fair enough," she said, tipping her glass in a mock toast before setting it back down. "But you can't stay on the fence forever, you know. That's just another way of keeping control."

You can't stay on the fence forever, her words replayed as I tried to process them, but they lodged themselves in my mind like splinters.

Annoying.

Persistent.

Impossible to ignore.

Reminding me that I needed to decide what I wanted and whether I was ready to reach for it, or if I'd let it slip through my fingers like so many other things.

9 / SOLÈNE

"You ready to end the night, butterfingers?"

"Hm?"

"I asked if you're ready to end the night..." Desiderio asked me as he led me out of the speakeasy. "Or if you want to spend some more time together."

I pulled my phone out of my bag to check the time.

1:57 AM.

Though a part of me wanted to call it a night, another part of me didn't want it to end. I was having the most fun with him that I had in ages, and the thought of going home now would feel like shutting a book halfway through a thrilling chapter, the kind you never want to put down.

And I found myself becoming addicted.

Looking down at my phone, I checked the time again.

1:59 AM.

Twelve texts from the group chat, asking me to update them on how my night was going. Quickly unlocking my phone to shoot the group chat message, I typed out, *Still alive. I'm having fun. Don't wait up.*

"They're wondering if I killed you yet?"

I slid my phone back into my bag. "Nope. Just being nosy.

Asking me what time I'll be home since I got Pilates at noon tomorrow."

"Yun's right?"

"Yup. Every Saturday," I looked up at him, smiling. "You really do pay attention."

He grinned. "I do."

"So," he continued as he stopped at the bottom of the speakeasy home's steps. "What's the verdict? Do we call it here and I call you an Uber, or do we let it stretch just a little longer?"

"I could go either way," I shrugged. "Depends on what you have in mind."

"Gotta make the decision," he said, stepping closer, his eyes lit with a playful challenge. "'Cause if you leave it up to me, I'm gonna decide to keep you out till the sun comes up."

"Well," I tilted my head, my heart somersaulting in my chest at his maddening smirk. "You haven't convinced me yet."

He feigned offense. "Oh, so now I gotta convince you? After spending the last couple of hours charming you?"

"Mhm."

His grin grew wider as he took a step closer.

"Bet," Desi said, his voice dropping just enough to make my pulse quicken. He dipped his head a little, locking me in that gaze of his that felt less like looking and more like falling. In that moment, my body betrayed me and leaned in closer, closing the gap he'd left hanging like an invitation. My mind spoke incoherent thoughts—drawing up scenarios a lady shouldn't entertain, my pulse roared in my ears, and my breath hitched when his hand brushed against mine.

His smirk deepened.

Without breaking eye contact, he slipped his fingers between mine, as though it had been made to fit just there. His thumb brushed against my knuckles in a simple, absent-minded motion that sent shivers racing up my spine.

Kiss him, my mind whispered when he looked down at my lips, then back up at my eyes.

Kiss him.

Kiss him.

KISS HIM.

But my lips didn't dare form the thought.

Instead, I chewed the inside of my cheek, trying to play it cool, though every fiber of my being was begging me to throw caution —and perhaps dignity—to the wind.

"You know," he murmured, his thumb still tracing lazy patterns on my hand, "If I didn't know any better, I'd say you were thinking about kissing me."

"That's a lie," my voice came out weaker than I intended, barely above a whisper, but he heard it.

Of course he did.

He tilted his head, leaning in so close that our lips almost touched, but not close enough to satisfy.

"Oh word?" I felt his breath graze my lips. "You sure about that, Butterfingers?"

I swallowed hard, my knees threatening to buckle beneath me.

"Positive," I whispered, though the word trembled at the edges, betraying me once again.

For a moment, he didn't move, just hovered there, his lips so tantalizingly close that my heart seemed to forget how to beat in rhythm. His eyes searched mine, like he was daring me to crack.

"Y'know," he murmured. "I don't think I believe you."

His lips twitched upward into that maddening smirk again, the kind that could both infuriate me and make my knees wobble all at once. He leaned back just enough to study me, to drink in the way I fumbled to keep my composure under his gaze.

And damn it, I was failing miserably.

"I'm a pretty good reader of people," he continued, his tone teasing but his eyes darker now, more serious than they had been all night, "and right now? You're looking at me like you want me to kiss you."

"I'm not—"

He stepped closer again, cutting off my words. His thumb

traced one last slow circle against my knuckles before his fingers tightened around mine, grounding me while simultaneously setting me adrift.

"Don't finish that sentence, mami," he whispered, his voice laced with a challenge I wasn't sure I could rise to. The world around us blurred—the distant hum of the bodega's music down the block, the faint laughter of late-night revelers passing by—everything faded into nothingness.

It was just him, his eyes locking on mine like a dare, his presence swallowing up.

"I dare you," he finished, his voice barely louder than a breath, "to tell me I'm wrong."

My throat clenched shut against any semblance of words, because if I finished my sentence, it would be a lie. My lips parted instinctively, but no sound came out.

Just breath—shallow, uneven—disobedient to my attempts at composure.

He had me right where he wanted me, and I knew it.

He knew it too.

A slow grin teased its way across his face as he tilted his head ever so slightly. "That's what I thought."

Before I had time to process it—to overthink my way out of this moment—he leaned in. His lips brushed against mine, so light and fleeting that heat exploded through me like lightning striking the same spot twice.

It wasn't enough.

It was too much.

My breath caught in my throat as he smirked against my lips; my common sense vanished into thin air like it never existed.

"Tell me to stop."

I couldn't.

The words didn't exist in me anymore.

My heart beat in double time, drowning out all thought except for the pull of him—this magnetic force that I was powerless to resist.

"Didn't think so," he murmured, and then his lips found mine, this time with no hesitation, no disruptions, no teasing trace. The kiss was gentle at first, like opening notes of an Anthony Hamilton love song, smooth and soulful, carrying a rhythm that drew me in deeper with every passing second.

But then, as if some silent crescendo demanded it, everything shifted.

The kiss deepened, and every inch of restraint I had left crumbled under the touch. His free hand found the curve of my waist, pulling me closer like he couldn't stand even the smallest distance between us anymore. No longer able to stay idle, my hands found their way to the back of his neck, and I weaved my fingers into his hair as I tilted my head to meet him more fully. The world slipped further away as I gave in to the kiss, letting it consume me completely. His touch was intoxicating, a perfect balance of careful control and unapologetic hunger.

Time seemed irrelevant, the rhythm of our kiss dictating everything instead. My mind was a riot of sensation—his scent, the warmth of his hands, the velvet press of his lips against mine. The city could've crumbled into dust around us, and I wouldn't have noticed.

When he finally pulled back, it was slow, hesitant, like he wasn't quite ready to let go, and neither was I. His forehead rested gently against mine, our breaths mingling in the small space between us. My pulse still thundered in my ears, drowning out everything except the memory of his lips on mine. His hand lingered at my waist, fingers curling slightly as if he was reluctant to break the connection.

"Well," his voice was soft and a little breathless. "That settles it. I'm not calling it a night. Not yet anyways."

I laughed quietly, my chest still heaving for air.

"There's this spot on Lexington and 76th near my—" his brows furrowed, and he looked up at the sky. "Did you feel that?"

"Feel what—" I was interrupted by a soft, cool droplet landing on my cheek. Then another followed, bringing a cascade of rain that came out of nowhere, catching us completely off guard.

"Change of plans," he said, running a hand through his now drenched curls as we moved under the awning of a nearby store-front. "Actually... I got a better idea."

10 / DESIDERIO

Did I feel like a pendejo for inviting her to my place so we could wait out the rain until our next adventure?

Probably.

However, I wasn't thinking straight.

Drunk off the kiss we just shared, I barely managed to form a coherent thought, let alone question my own decisions. My mind was on some lovestruck loop, my hands still felt like static from holding her, and my heartbeat currently matched the speed of a Toyota Camry racing on the freeway.

Ay mami.

The things this woman was doing to me without realizing it.

First, it was me noticing the subtle things to figure her out. Now, it was me throwing caution to the wind, letting her into my space—where every corner told a story I haven't shared with anyone else other than family.

Mierda. I'm losing control, but... I don't care.

I didn't care because it was for her. Liked her too damn much to stop myself.

I wanted her all to myself.

"I couldn't find the hair dryer, so I'm gonna let my hair air-dry," I heard her say as she came out of the guest bedroom.

"It should be in the cabinet unless my sister—"

Pausing as she appeared in the hallway, she wore the lime green Sade shirt and Celtics basketball shorts I left behind for her. It hung loosely to her frame, swallowing all her curves, yet somehow making her look even more irresistible. My throat tightened as I took in the sight of her—bare-faced, coils damp and curling around her cheeks and shoulders, looking utterly at home in my clothes.

Ay. I gulped, nodding like some damn dog begging for scraps.

"Unless your sister what?"

"Oh... Uh," I scratched the back of my neck. "Uh—I mean, I think one of my sisters took it the last time they were here."

"You okay?" she asked, tilting her head slightly to the side.

My mouth suddenly dried up, and my tongue felt like it was glued to the roof of it.

Okay? Hell no, I wasn't okay.

I was a grown man, and yet here I was, unraveling just because she looked like she belonged here.

Like she belonged with me.

I watched as her eyes narrowed slightly.

Mierda.

Scrambling for words, I felt like a fucking pendejo again, my tongue heavy and useless in my mouth.

"Yeah, yeah," I managed to croak out. "You look good. Comfortable."

My attempt at nonchalance fell flat; the chuckle she gave in response told me as much.

Dios mío.

Focus, cabrón. Focus.

"Thanks for the shirt, by the way. It's like five sizes too big for me, but I appreciate it," she teased, tugging on the hem of the shirt that only just grazed her hips. The movement pulled the fabric tighter over her collarbone for a second, giving me a preview of her pebbled nipples against the cotton...

Wait... are her nipples pierced?

I quickly took another peek while she tugged the shirt, her attention on the print of Sade's face on the front.

Carajo.

Yep, there was no denying it.

Tiny heart-shaped bars under the cotton—clear as day now.

Heart-shaped piercings.

Why didn't I notice them before? We were together all day, and her dress wasn't thick enough to hide them, and we were pressed so close when kissing...

My throat felt tighter, a lump climbing up to lodge itself firmly there as I tried to redirect my thoughts.

But every time I blinked, the image was burned into my brain —the soft curve of her chest under my shirt, the delicate outline of those tiny hearts teasing me like they had a world of secrets to whisper in my ear...

Or my mouth.

Focus, focus, ***focus.***

I blinked hard, fighting to keep my eyes from wandering back down.

"Desi?"

"Yeah, uh... sure, no problem," I said, clearing my throat and looking away, pretending the window suddenly looked fascinating. "You can wear it until your clothes are all good to go."

She squinted.

"Are you sure you're okay? You look nervous..." she said, leaning one shoulder against the hallway wall. Her arms crossed loosely over her chest, which only managed to draw more attention to everything I was trying—and failing—not to look at.

"Nervous?" I laughed awkwardly, scratching the back of my neck again like an idiot. "Nah, not at all."

Her brows arched. "You really sure? 'Cause you're acting like you've never had a woman wear a hoodie of yours or something before."

"I mean... I never did so..." I muttered, my eyes darting away again.

She blinked, her teasing smirk faltering for a second. "Wait, really?"

Heat crept up the back of my neck and spread over my ears.

Damn it.

Why couldn't I have left it at an eye roll or cracked a joke? Anything but admitting **that**.

"Yeah..." I shrugged, trying not to let the weight of her gaze make me crumble. “Unless you count my sisters who love to steal my shit.”

Her lips parted slightly, and for a moment, the only sound in the room was the soft patter of rain against the living room windows overlooking Lexington Ave & E 86th St. She uncrossed her arms and pushed herself off the wall.

"Oh... I guess there’s a first time for everything," she nodded, then bit her lip.

"Guess you're right."

Walking over to my dark green togo sectional, I watched as she plopped on it like it was her own, folding her legs underneath her. One hand moved to adjust the curls falling into her face, and the other fidgeted with the hem of the oversized shirt.

"Your place is... not what I expected," she glanced around, taking in my bookshelves filled with art books and vinyls. My walls were lined with Black and Latin art I collected since college, and framed photos of me and my family.

"Why? What'd you expect?" I asked, trying to sound relaxed as I leaned against the kitchen archway, my hands in the pockets of my sweatpants, which I just threw on.

She laughed softly, a sound so low and sweet it made something inside me unravel even further. "I don't know—I guess too manly? Bachelor-pad like? Maybe some random dude stuff like a poster of a Lamborghini or whatever. But this though..." she reached for the open furniture book on the monti coffee table, her fingers skimming over the worn cover. “This is... your place is well thought out. It’s beautiful.”

“And the art,” she continued as she looked back at the walls, her gaze lingering on a framed print of a colorful market scene from Santo Domingo, which I took on vacation. "It feels intentional, like every piece has a story."

I didn't know what to say to that, so I just nodded, my brain still caught somewhere between the way she looked in my clothes and the way her lips formed every word.

"That's a good thing, right?"

She smiled again. "Oh yeah. Definitely a good thing."

For a brief moment, we fell into silence again, but it wasn't uncomfortable. The rain outside softened to a gentle rhythm, almost as if it slowed down just for us.

Shifting her weight on the couch, she tucked her legs under herself in a way that made her look even smaller in my clothes. Her fingers continued playing idly with the edges of the furniture book before flipping it open to a page filled with a bunch of mid-century chair designs. Her brow furrowed a bit as she studied the glossy photographs like she was trying to piece together my entire personality from the objects.

"You really surprise me," she said suddenly, not looking up. Though her voice was casual, something in the way she said it made my chest tighten.

I pushed off the archway and walked closer, sitting close to her but not so close to lose my shit and do something like touch her. "How?"

Her lips quirked into a half-smile, still staring at the page like it held all the answers.

"Now that I'm in your home... I get a completely different vibe about you."

"Good or bad?"

"Good," She finally looked up, her eyes catching mine with more intensity than I was ready for. "I originally thought you were just confident, easygoing, maybe a little cocky." She paused, chewing on her bottom lip as if debating what to say next. "But now... I see more parts of you."

"And what are those parts?" I dug my fingers into the couch, keeping me grounded as my pulse kicked up a notch. Her gaze didn't waver, and that half-smile grew into something fuller, something that made it hard to breathe.

"Parts like..." she paused, tilting her head and narrowing her eyes at me playfully. "Like maybe you're a little more sensitive than you let on."

"Sensitive?"

"Mhm," she nodded. "That's why you're so observant. You pay attention to things so you don't miss things. You care in ways most people don't, even if you pretend it's no big deal."

"And you got all of that from..."

She laughed.

"Somewhat," she shut the book, leaning back into the couch. Her head tilted just slightly as she studied me again, this time with a curiosity that felt like she was seeing right through me. "Just calling it like I sees it."

I ran a hand over my mouth, trying to hide the small smile threatening to betray me.

Just like that, she had me again.

Saying things that'll have my mind replaying her words.

"So," she said after a moment of silence between us, leaning back against the couch and allowing herself to sink even deeper into its cushions as she looked around my living room. "What do you wanna do until the rain stops?"

Nothing PG rated.

"I don't know," I shrugged, trying my best not to stare at the way her collarbone peeked out from the loose neckline of my shirt, or the tiny bead of water still clinging to her skin like it didn't know where else to go. "I got—"

She quickly stood up and rushed towards my vinyl collection, pulling out a record before I could even finish my sentence.

"I can't believe you have this," she turned to me, holding out the Rose In The Dark vinyl I recently added to my collection.

"You like Cleo Soul?"

"Like her? You kidding me? I *love* her," she said, clutching the record to her chest like it was a holy relic. "This album got me through some of the toughest days last year."

I stood and walked over to join her by the shelf, my heart thudding louder with every step.

"Really? What song?"

She didn't answer right away; instead, she turned the record over in her hands, reading the tracklist as if she needed a reminder.

"Honestly? There's no way I can pick just one. 'When I'm In Your Arms' maybe? Or 'Young Love.'" She paused and glanced up at me with a soft smile that made my chest ache. "The way her voice wraps around you... It's like medicine for the soul."

"Yeah... It really is."

Her fingers skimmed over the edge of the vinyl case before she handed it to me. "Can we listen to it? Please?"

I took the album from her without hesitation and slid the vinyl from its sleeve. "Of course."

Walking over to my Fluance RT85N record player near the floor-to-ceiling windows, I carefully placed the vinyl on the turntable and purposefully placed the needle to start playing When I'm In Your Arms.

As the first few chords filled the room, her shoulders visibly relaxed, and she closed her eyes.

"You picked that song on purpose, didn't you?" she asked as her hips started swaying gently to the beat, her eyes still shut.

I leaned back against the edge of the shelf, crossing my arms as I watched her. Every movement she made was so effortless, so unguarded, like the music that poured out of the speakers was flowing straight through her veins. My pulse quickened again as I noticed the way her coils bounced with every sway of her head, and how the hem of my oversized shirt and shorts flirted with her thighs, revealing just a glimpse of smooth, brown skin each time she moved.

She was lost in the rhythm, and I was lost in her, my heart pounding against my ribcage with every step she took closer to the couch.

Her eyes blinking open, she caught me staring for what felt like the hundredth time that night. She didn't call me out this time, though. Instead, she grinned and moved closer to me to close the distance between us.

"You're doing it again," she looked up at me.

"Doing what?" I asked, though I already knew.

"Looking at me like..." She trailed off, searching my face with a sultry look that stopped my breath short. Her fingers reached out, brushing against my chest as if testing the waters. "Like that."

"Don't do that," I breathed out, taking my hands into hers.

She batted her eyelashes at me. "Don't do what?"

"That," I muttered, my throat dry as I held her hands. "Don't look at me like you don't know what you're doing. Like you don't know how hard it is for me not to..." My words trailed off, my resolve faltering under the weight of her gaze.

Her lips quirked up into a sly, knowing smile as she stepped even closer, leaving barely an inch between us. "Not to what?"

I closed my eyes for a moment, exhaling slowly.

This woman was testing every ounce of my self-control and making it feel effortless. The scent of her—vanilla and now thanks to my body wash cedar-wood, wrapped around me in waves, pulling me under before I could think straight.

"Not to kiss you again," I admitted finally, my voice low and uneven.

Her smile widened slightly, but her gaze softened as she tilted her head up to look at me. "What's stopping you?"

Her eyelids fluttered, but she didn't move back.

If anything, she leaned closer, the corners of her lips tugging upward in that playful way that made me weak.

"So why don't you?" she challenged softly, her breath grazing my jawline.

And just like that, it was over for me.

11 / SOLÈNE

SIDEWAYS BY CLEO SOUL playing in the background, his hand found the back of my neck as he brought my face to his. His lips brushed against mine like a question first, then, without warning, he searched for the answer on his own. Tongue mingling with my own, the taste of him was warm and intoxicating, like cinnamon and buttered rum tea on a cold night. The world around us blurred into nothing but the rhythm of our breath. His hands caressed every inch of my waist, fingers digging in possessively, and I surrendered without resistance.

"Fuuuck," he groaned into my mouth once my fingers found the nape of his neck, my nails drawing soft, deliberate patterns against his skin. Pulling me closer to him as if it was possible, his hands slid to my butt and he lifted me effortlessly without breaking the kiss. I gasped against his lips, my legs wrapping around him as he moved towards the couch. Once settled onto the cushions with me on his lap, he pulled away.

His eyes burned into mine, dark and heavy. My chest rose and fell erratically as I tried to catch my breath, my heart pounding like a war drum. I felt his dick print press against me through the barrier of our clothes as he took a deep, uneven breath. His lips, slightly parted, curved into the faintest smirk as he squeezed my waist.

"Why'd you stop?" I whispered. Some part of me was embarrassed by how desperate I sounded, but the larger part didn't care. Not when his thumb was brushing against my bottom lip, his gaze alternating between my mouth and my eyes like he couldn't decide which temptation was greater.

"'Cause I needa look at you," he murmured, his voice low and rough. His thumb lingered on my lip for a moment longer before trailing down my chin, his touch igniting sparks that traveled through every nerve in my body. "You're so fucking beautiful like this."

The words melted any remaining resolve I had, making my breath hitch as my cheeks flushed.

I didn't know what to say to that—what could I say?

Instead of fumbling for words, my fingers sneaked into his hair, tugging slightly, and it earned me a sharp intake of breath from him. That sound—sharp, needy, vulnerable—sent a jolt straight through me, pooling heat low in my belly.

"You don't play fair," I managed to whisper, though my voice was unsteady. "You haven't played fair all night."

"Oh word?"

"Word," I shot back.

His smirk widened, a dangerous curve that promised he knew exactly the effect he had on me. "I never said I wanted to."

His hands slid under the shirt, palms skimming over my sides before settling high on my ribs, his thumbs brushing just under the curve of my breasts. His eyes searching mine, he didn't move further, however, just lingered there. My body decided before my mind could, I tried leaning into him to continue the kiss, but he stopped me with a gentle, teasing pressure against my hip.

"Uh-uh," he murmured, his voice a velvet rasp that made my stomach flutter. "Not yet."

"Why?"

"I wanna have your consent before I..." his voice trailed off. His hands stayed steady as his eyes scanned my face. "We just met hours ago and..."

I nodded. "We did."

"I don't wanna rush you," he exhaled. "It doesn't mean I don't want you—hell, it couldn't be clearer how much I do—but I wanna know... I needa know you're good with this."

My chest constricted at his words, his vulnerability carving a space in my heart I wasn't ready to admit existed.

Desi was unlike anyone I'd met before.

Though he was the first man I've gone another *date* with outside of my ex, his hesitation reminded me of a care I hadn't known I longed for. Everything about this man was pure intention—something I craved yet never got the opportunity to experience.

He paid attention to the little things, he valued my opinions all the while... And now, here he was, with me sitting on his lap, waiting for an answer. He could've easily kept going, peeling away my resolve like the layers of an onion, but he didn't.

Instead, he chose to ask, to reassure me that my choice mattered.

This was the kind of conscientiousness that made my heart ache in the best way.

Boy, was I falling... *hard.*

Because how could I not fall for someone like him? Someone who looked at me like I was the only woman in the world and treated me with so much respect and patience I didn't know I was capable of receiving.

However, I had to remind myself that I had no clue where the night would end.

It didn't matter how much I felt myself slipping into him, I was still faced with the unknown. Desi was here now—yes—but he wasn't forever. Not when we haven't even discussed how we plan to move forward from tonight. Not when I had no idea what he really wanted from this, or if he even thought there was a future for us beyond this fleeting, magnetic connection.

For all I knew, this could just be a perfect moment in an

imperfect world—one of those memories you hold onto when the nights are too quiet and too long.

So I had to accept tonight as a *live-in-the-moment* kind of thing. I wasn't going to ruin it by asking what might come next.

That would be a worry for when our time ended.

His voice broke through my thoughts. "What're you thinking?"

I bit my lip, however, he removed one of his hands from under my shirt, using his thumb to gently tug my lip free before it went back to its resting place.

"Don't do that. I want to know what you're thinking," he urged. "If you're not okay with this, we can stop—"

"I'm good," I said softly, my fingers still tangled gently in his hair. "I want this, too."

"Are you sure?"

"Yeah..."

His exhale trembled against my cheek, and for a brief moment, his eyes closed as though he was trying to absorb my reply. When he opened them again, they were darker somehow, deeper, like whatever restraint he had been holding onto had loosened its grip.

"Good," he rasped, planting a quick kiss on my lips before pulling away to stare at me. "I need you to tell me if it ever changes."

I ignored the way my heart hammered against my ribcage, leaning in again to brush my lips against his, but he shook his head.

"Promise me, Solène," he whispered my name like a prayer, and it sent a shiver down my spine. "Promise me you'll tell me if it ever becomes too much."

"I promise."

"Okay then," he murmured, his lips curling into a faint smile as his thumb traced slow circles against my waist. "Then let me take my time with you."

12 / SOLÈNE

HE MOVED SLOWLY like he was savoring every second.

His fingers sliding up my sides, he took the hem of the shirt with them until it slipped over my head and onto the floor. The cool air kissed my skin, making me shiver as his gaze roamed over me unhurried. His hands followed the path of his eyes, tracing the curve of my shoulders, the line of my collarbone, until they settled right on my chest.

His thumbs brushed over the peak of each mound as though he were memorizing me by touch. My breath hitched, the warmth of his palms branding me, and yet his movements remained reverent—like I was something sacred. His lips parted slightly, and for a heartbeat, I thought he might say something. Instead, they descended on the hollow of my throat, pressing soft, lingering kisses along the sensitive skin there. My pulse fluttered beneath his mouth like a bird desperate to take flight.

"Desi," his name escaped me in a moan so soft I barely heard it myself.

He froze, pulling from my neck to meet my eyes.

"Say that again." It wasn't a demand or even a request. It was more like a plea from somewhere deep inside him.

My lips parted as his thumb toyed with the heart-shaped piercing on my left nipple. "Desi..."

He closed his eyes and groaned. Before I could process, his hands found the center of my back as he leaned me backwards on his lap. Head tilted back, my hair spilled over my shoulders as I arched into him, gasping softly when his lips found the center of my chest. His tongue darted out to trace lazy, torturous patterns down the valley between my breasts.

"Watch me," he rasped against my skin as he took one of my nipples into his mouth, his tongue swirling over the delicate metal of the piercing. My eyes fluttered shut instinctively, but his low growl of disapproval brought me back to attention.

"I said, watch me," he repeated, tugging onto the hardened peak gently with his teeth before releasing it, which sent an electric jolt to my pussy. My eyes snapped open, locking onto his as he gazed at me from beneath heavy lids.

Satisfied that he had my attention by the smirk on his face, his mouth returned to my chest and worked skillfully. His lips alternated between kisses, sucks and grazes of his teeth, as though he was learning to play me like an instrument. Every touch was a note, every moan was a melody. Unable to stop myself, my hands clutched at his shoulders, fingers digging into the taut muscles. His grip on my back tightened ever so slightly as I shifted against him, instinctively seeking out more of him. The slow grind of my hips against his lap drew a rumble from his chest, pulling him away from my skin just long enough to shoot me a look that was equal parts warning and hunger.

Rising from the couch in one swift motion, he carried me effortlessly in his arms. My breath caught as my limbs instinctively clung to him, his strength and the deliberate purpose in his movements sending a thrill through me. He strode toward his hallway, his eyes never leaving mine as he nudged the halfway open bedroom door. Inside revealed a dimly lit sanctuary of an upholstered bed covered in charcoal-grey sheets in the center. Beside it were matching nightstands with soft glowing lamps and a small stack of books on the one by the floor-to-ceiling windows that cast a faint reflection of the two of us entwined.

Door closed off to the music in the living room, he set me down gently on the edge of the bed, his hands never once leaving my body as though afraid I might disappear if he let go. His thumbs grazed over my thighs, kneading softly as his eyes drank me in.

"Lie back," he murmured, and I obeyed without hesitation, leaning back against the cool sheets, my head resting on one of the plush pillows. I watched as he slipped out of his shirt and sweatpants, revealing a sculpted frame that made my breath catch and my lower lips throb. The soft lights from the bedside lamps danced across his skin, highlighting every ridge and contour. My eyes trailed down the ridges of his abs, the sharp cut of his hips, and the hard lines of his shoulders as he stood there for a moment, his gaze locked on me.

Fuck was this man blessed down below.

"Can I do something?" I breathed as I slowly pulled myself up on my elbows. His brows lifted slightly in curiosity, but then he smirked.

"You can do anything you want to me, Solène."

Slowly, like a predator closing in on its prey, I slid forward on the bed until I was on my knees, my body barely inches from his. My hands found his sides, tracing the defined lines of his torso with featherlight touches, reveling in the way his muscles tensed beneath my palms. His breath hitched as I leaned in closer, pressing a kiss to the center of his chest. My lips lingered there for a moment before trailing lower, leaving a path of soft kisses and teasing nips along his skin.

His hands fell to my damp coils, tangling gently in the strands while he exhaled a deep, guttural sound as my lips found his hips. I paused, my breath fanning warm against his skin, and glanced up at him through my lashes. His eyes were half-lidded, jaw clenched as his fingers tightened in my hair, like he was holding himself back.

Now the one to smirk, my fingers took his curved girth into a slow, tentative grip, marveling at the heat and weight of him. A groan escaped his lips as I took my time, letting my tongue trace a slow, deliberate circle over his oozing tip before pulling back slightly to meet his gaze. His breathing hitched, and with every flick of my tongue, every teasing movement, I could feel the tension building in him like a storm ready to break.

"Stop driving me insane—fuuuck!" he moaned, his voice breaking as I took him deeper, my lips wrapping around his dick deliberately. His hips bucked slightly, but he forced himself to still as his hand pulled at my coils. I moved at my own pace, savoring every reaction that escaped him: the way his breathing grew more ragged with every flick of my tongue, the soft curses that spilled from his lips when I tightened my grip around the base. His fingers trembled in my hair; his restraint was hanging by a thread, and it thrilled me to know that I was the one unraveling him.

"Solène," he growled. "You're gonna make me—fuck—I'm—"

Taking his plea as encouragement to pick up the pace, I hollowed my cheeks and moved deeper, drawing a strangled sound from his chest. My fingers played with his base, stroking in tandem with the ministrations of my mouth, which snapped his control. With a rough moan, he pulled me away, a string of saliva still connecting me to him as I panted for breath.

"You don't play fair," he tried to say between heavy breaths.

I looked up at him, batting my lashes innocently. "I don't want to."

"Fine," he sucked his teeth. "Then neither will I."

In one swift moment, his hand holding my hair guided me back up to his eye level. His lips crashed against mine more hungrily, the kiss consuming the breath from my lungs. My eyes closed as I melted into him, his hand gripping my ass with newfound urgency. I barely had time to react before he picked me back up and pushed me against the cool white wall. My back met the smooth surface with a thud. I wrapped my legs around him as his hips pressed into mine. The hard, solid feel of him grinding against my core made me gasp, and he took the opportunity to slip his tongue into my mouth, deepening the kiss until it felt like the world outside had disappeared entirely. His hands moved to cup the curve of my thighs, lifting me higher, and I felt a finger swipe at my soaked folds.

Breaking the kiss, he kept me hoisted in the air with one hand as the other found his mouth, slipping his finger coated in my wetness.

“Mhmm,” a groan escaped his throat as he tasted me. “You taste exactly how I imagined you would.”

Sliding his hand back down, I whimpered as he played along my folds again before dipping them inside. My head fell back against the wall, and I cried out softly as his fingers curled within, hitting that spot with unerring precision. Every stroke sent ripples of pleasure radiating through my body like the pull of a tide intent on drowning me in desire.

“You make the prettiest sounds,” he murmured against my neck as his fingers worked relentlessly. His lips found the tender spot just below my ear, teeth grazing lightly before he sucked the skin softly, marking in a way that felt possessive. My hips rolled against his hand instinctively, chasing the delicious friction as he teased me closer and closer to the edge.

“Desiiii,” I moaned, my voice trembling as I felt my orgasm near. He withdrew his fingers, leaving me gasping and trembling in his arms, teetering on the brink of release. My eyes flew open to meet his intense gaze.

"Not yet, mami... I want to feel you fall apart around me."

Reaching over to the dresser, he grabbed a condom from the top drawer without breaking eye contact. He tore the wrapper with his teeth while I watched his every move with bated breath, my sex dripping with need. Effortlessly rolling the condom on, he positioned himself between my legs.

“Ready for me, mami?”

I nodded breathlessly, but that wasn’t enough for him. He dipped his head closer, his lips brushing lightly against mine. “Words, Solène.”

"Yes," I gasped. "Yes, Desi."

With a slow, deliberate thrust, he entered me, the stretch stealing what little breath I had left. My head tipped back against the wall as we both moaned. He filled me completely, stretching me with an exquisite ache that bordered on ecstasy. My nails dug into his shoulders as I clung to him; I needed to anchor myself, or else I'd lose all sense of reality. His forehead pressed against mine, our breaths mingling as we shared the same rhythm, shared this intimate connection born out of something far more profound than lust alone.

"Te sientes mejor de lo que yo imaginé,*" he whispered as he adjusted his hold on me.

Then he began to move.

His thrusts were slow at first, deliberate and deep, as though he wanted to imprint every inch of himself into me. Each motion sent a shockwave through my body, drawing out soft, uncontrollable whimpers from my lips. My breasts bounced against his chest with every deliberate roll of his hips, the friction between us building like a fire threatening to consume everything. His lips found my neck again, planting open-mouthed kisses along the column of my throat, each one branding me in ways I couldn't explain. The rhythm of his movements remained steady, controlled, though I could feel the tension coiling tighter and tighter within him.

"Desi..." I moaned again, my voice fractured, needy. His name was all I could manage, my thoughts dissolving into the haze of sensation he created in me.

"Say it again," he demanded against my skin, the gruffness of his tone sending another wave of heat pooling between my thighs. His hips snapped forward, harder this time, the rhythm shifting from patient to insistent. "Say my name like that, mami."

Unable to deny him anything at this moment, I cried out for him louder this time.

---

* *Te sientes mejor de lo que yo imaginé = you feel better than I imagined*

Delivering one brutal thrust that had me seeing stars, he quickly maneuvered me from the wall to his bed. The rhythm of his hips never faltered as he laid me down, it became rougher, more erratic, each thrust punctuated by guttural groans that vibrated against my mouth. My fingernails scraped down his back as he drove into me with a passion that held nothing back. Every roll of his hips pushed me closer to the edge, every deep stroke unraveling me piece by piece. My world narrowed to the feel of him—his weight pressing me into the mattress, his breath hot against my neck, his relentless pace stealing every coherent thought from my brain. I clenched around him involuntarily, drawing a choked moan from his lips as he buried himself deeper.

"Mírate..." he licked along the shell of my ear. ""Tan hermosa cuando estás así."*

His words—though I didn't understand—sent a shiver racing down my spine, the timbre of his voice wrapping around me like the most intimate caress. My body arched beneath him, desperate for more as his pace grew increasingly erratic, every thrust dragging against that perfect spot inside me that had me seeing constellations.

I moaned again his name, clawing at his back as he drove me to oblivion. He gripped my thighs hard enough to anchor me, holding me exactly where he wanted as he pulled back just enough to look down at me.

"Dios mío," he groaned through gritted teeth. "You're squeezing me so tight... you feel like heaven, mami." His gaze roamed over me once again, dark and brimming with raw intensity. The slick slide of our bodies, the sound of skin slapping against skin, and the sound of our breathing filled the room like a symphony.

Without warning, I broke apart under him, my entire body locking up as pleasure exploded in waves so powerful it left me

---

* *Mírate... tan hermosa cuando estás así = Look at yourself... so beautiful when you're like this.*

trembling and gasping for air. His name fell from my lips in a litany, an unending mantra of devotion.

Desi followed me into the abyss, a low growl tearing from his throat as he buried himself deep one final time. His body shuddered against mine, his grip on my thighs tightening as his own release overwhelmed him. He pressed his forehead to mine, our breaths mingling in a chaotic, fragile rhythm, both of us trying to steady ourselves in the aftermath of what had just unraveled between us.

The room fell quiet save for the sound of our ragged breathing and the rain outside the windows. His weight pressed down on me—a comforting, grounding sensation rather than oppressive—and I let my hands travel lazily up his back, feeling the faint sheen of sweat on his skin.

“I didn’t hurt you, did I?”

My lips quivered into a soft smile, still catching my breath as I shook my head. "No.”

“Good,” he kissed the top of my head, withdrawing from me slowly, the absence of him leaving a strange ache in my belly. He removed the condom carefully, discarding it in the small trash bin by the nightstand before collapsing beside me. His arm sliding in between my legs, he pulled me against him, tucking me securely into his side like I belonged there.

I let out a yawn. “Desi—”

“Sleep,” he kissed the top of my head once more. “We’ll talk later, mami. For now, just rest.”

I wanted to protest, a dozen words dancing on the tip of my tongue, but the exhaustion in my body, coupled with the soothing rhythm of his heartbeat against my ear, stole any rebuttal I might’ve had. His fingers traced gentle patterns along my back, a wordless lullaby that made it almost impossible to resist the pull of sleep.

So I surrendered to the darkness, melting into the warmth of him.

13 / SOLÈNE

I WOKE up refreshed like no other.

An itch scratched, and the air suddenly felt easier to breathe. Any lingering weight that my ex had left behind had been lifted. Last night with Desi was wonderful, and I couldn't stop the smile tugging at my lips as I replayed the moments. Like a rainbow blossoming after a long storm, it erased every trace that burrowed into the corners of my mind, giving me the fresh romantic start I yearned for.

The weight I'd carried for months was no more.

Making me wonder how I had ever been content settling for less.

I had tasted what it felt like to be truly seen, truly heard, and I couldn't go back to pretending otherwise.

Now, I just hoped that Desi felt the same way.

The sound of birds chirping outside his window added a cheery soundtrack to my morning thoughts. Sunlight streamed in through the curtains, painting soft golden patches on the hardwood floor. I stretched lazily, savoring the warmth of his comforter for a moment longer before my hands reached the other side of the bed, hoping to find him still there. Meeting emptiness, my smile faltered, just a notch, as my fingers brushed against the crisp sheet.

Hm.

The clock on his nightstand blinked 9:47 AM. I sat up slowly, letting the blanket fall away as I stretched again. Straining my ear to listen, I heard no movement. The room still carried faint traces of him: the scent of his cologne mingling with the clean smell of freshly washed sheets. Curiosity nudged at me as I swung my legs over the edge of the bed and stood, the wooden floor cool against my bare feet.

Had he left for an early errand?

Gym maybe?

Hm.

He went to grab—

I paused, noticing my clothes and a couple of things neatly folded on a durango lounge chair with my bag by it. The sight made my chest tighten.

Words caught in my throat, tight and tangled like an overgrown vine. My eyes lingered too long on the perfectly arranged pile, as if studying it would unravel some hidden meaning. The air seemed to shift, just slightly replaced by something heavier, unspoken.

A note. *There has to be a note.*

I looked around his room for a note in hopes of making sense of his absence or the sudden ease pooling at the base of my stomach, yet found none.

Was this... purposeful?

No, that wasn't right.

Desi wasn't like that.

But Naomi had told me: "If a man takes the time to fold your clothes after a one-night stand, he's trying to keep you at arm's length."

Her voice echoed in my mind, the way it always did when she said something observant and maddeningly correct. I shook her words off, convinced that her jaded perspective couldn't possibly apply to Desi. He wasn't like the others she's experienced. His kindness wasn't a façade; he didn't seem like the type to overthink his actions or play games.

He was too observant for this.

Too intentional.

Every move last night he made felt deliberate... So why did this feel like something entirely different?

Still, standing there in his room, surrounded by traces of him but no presence to match—it made me uneasy. I didn't want to overthink it, and didn't want to let Naomi's skeptical tone claw its way into my good mood. But something about the way my belongings were so carefully laid out whispered planning more than happenstance.

This was unknown territory for me, considering that this was my first time having a one-night stand... ever.

Maybe I was jumping to conclusions. Maybe he had something urgent that needed his attention—something he hadn't anticipated.

The silence in the apartment felt heavier now, pressing against my chest. I passed my hand over my dress, my fingers twitching like they couldn't decide what to do next. A dull ache bloomed at the base of my throat.

Still, the what-ifs clawed at me.

I glanced toward the window. The sunlight hadn't shifted much, but it suddenly felt too bright, too sharp.

Was it too much to hope he'd left a small gesture, a message of reassurance?

Maybe I should call Naomi and ask her about this.

Reaching for my phone, I unlocked the screen and searched for my best friend's name, but my thumb hesitated above the call button.

What was I even going to say? That I'd had a perfect night, woke up feeling ecstatic, and then immediately spiraled into doubt because of a neatly folded pile of clothes? Naomi would laugh, then lecture me about overthinking. She wouldn't mean it unkindly, but still—it wasn't what I needed right now.

I set the phone down on the edge of the chair and exhaled slowly.

Maybe I was overreacting. Maybe Desi was just... considerate.

Folding my clothes didn't automatically mean he was trying to put distance between us, right? It could just as easily be him being thoughtful, making sure I didn't wake up to a mess.

That sounded like something he'd do.

Remaking myself comfortable on the bed, I stared at the ceiling for what felt like forever, my mind twisting in circles as I tried to make sense of the quiet. The logical part of me wanted to trust his intentions, to chalk this up to a simple morning errand or a caring gesture. But the softer, more vulnerable side of me—the one that had experienced too many disappointments before—nudged at the unease still lingering in my chest.

Unable to stay still, I got up again, wrapping his bedsheets around me before padding out into the hallway. The apartment was bathed in that soft morning light, every detail illuminated—his bookshelves, the art on the walls, two mismatched mugs stacked neatly by the sink. I moved toward the kitchen, my bare feet making almost inaudible sounds against the hardwood. My focus darted to the counter, searching for a note, a scribble—anything that might say more than this silence offered.

But there was nothing.

Just the stillness.

I chewed on my bottom lip, the consumption of uncertainty now dampening the high I woke up with.

Was I not worthy of a simple explanation? A word or two on a piece of paper?

Had I misread everything?

Was last night just that—a fleeting moment he wanted to wrap up neatly and put away?

That wasn't Desi—not from what I knew of him so far. He had been nothing but kind, attentive even, and our connection last night wasn't the kind you just tucked away and forgot... Was I wrong to think it meant more?

Then again… maybe I was wrong about a lot of things.

It wouldn't be the first time.

Back inside the room again, I stared at the neatly folded pile, my fingers brushing over the fabric absentmindedly.

He folded my clothes.

The realization hit me like a drop of cold water sliding down my spine.

Desiderio folded my clothes.

That already told me more than any words could have, and I needed to accept what it meant.

It wasn't a careless toss, an afterthought, or a rushed gesture. It was deliberate. Thoughtful, even. But thoughtful in a way that suddenly felt distant, measured, and maybe even too polite. It made me understand that he didn't see me the way I had started to see him. Last night for him was a neatly packaged and compartmentalized fleeting moment, like the clothes on his chair.

And that was okay for me. That *had* to be okay for me.

Despite the smile I had worn since waking up fading, despite my chest feeling tight in a way I couldn't name, I was going to be alright because I didn't regret a second of it. Last night was exactly what I needed to remind me of who I was, of what I deserved. It didn't matter if Desi didn't see things the same way. For once, I wasn't living my life based on someone's validation.

I had already found something I didn't realize I'd been searching for: clarity.

Letting out a sigh, I grabbed the items off the nightstand and started dressing.

Time for the fairytale to end, I suppose.

14 / SOLÈNE

"LET ME GET THIS RIGHT," Naomi's voice cracked slightly as she raised an incredulous eyebrow. "You just left... after everything that you told us happened last night?"

Propping my phone against my bedroom's large brown dresser, I chewed on my bottom lip. "Yeah..."

"This bitch—" Naomi sighed, dragging her palm down her face dramatically. "I—" she sighed. "What the hell is wrong with you?"

"Allie, Lizzy," I looked at my other friends on the FaceTime call as I slipped into my dark blue sportswear for pilates. "Am I wrong for leaving?"

Before Alexandra or Elizabeth could reply, Naomi screamed. "Yes!"

"But–"

"You assumed and then left!" She jabbed a finger at the screen like she could physically smack some sense into me through our FaceTime call. "You didn't even have a talk with him. You didn't get any kind of closure, nor did you even try to understand what the hell was going on!"

Alexandra leaned closer on her end, tucking a strand of her jet black hair behind her ear. "You know I never side with Naomi buuuuuuut it's a little dramatic to just leave without saying anything instead of waiting for an explanation—"

"What explanation justifies that?" Elizabeth interrupted, her sharp tone cutting across Alexandra's calm reasoning. Her perfectly arched brow furrowed as she stared into the camera. "You wake up to clothes folded neatly? No thanks. I'd be out too."

Naomi sucked her teeth. "Liz, you've never had a one-night stand, nor have you ever woken up to anything less than sunshine and daisies 'cause your boyfriend gives you the world. Your opinion doesn't count here."

"It does if I know that girl code 101 is that if you find your clothes like *that,*" Elizabeth shot back. "It's clear as day that you needa gooooo. Your stay has been overextended, sis. You gotta bounce. No questions asked. No need to stick around for the awkward conversation. Plus, he's a Dominican man from the Bronx... that's a red flag right there," she finished, crossing her arms triumphantly.

"Oh lord," Alexandra groaned. "Not this again..."

Naomi groaned, throwing both hands in the air. "Oh my God, Liz, not this Bronx slander again! One time—literally one time—a Bronx guy ghosted you, and now they're all villains?"

"Yes," Elizabeth nodded. "I stand ten toes on what I said."

Naomi grimaced, throwing her head back dramatically before snapping forward again to glare at the screen.

"So he can't be considerate?!" She jabbed her finger once more. "Thoughtful?!"

"You know what?" Alexandra pursed her red lips. "Tony did have a thing for folding y'all's clothes which I found weird buuuut... that was his thing. Remember that time he folded all your laundry while waiting for you to get ready?"

Naomi clapped her hands together in disbelief, leaning closer to the screen. "Exactly! Thank you, Allie! That's what I'm saying. What if he was just being NICE? Like, 'Hey, let me make sure she doesn't wake up in a pile of random-ass clothes'.

Besides, what kind of man nowadays goes out of their way to fold clothes for a woman he doesn't like? Most men would have your ass out as soon as he nutted. Or he'll have your shit in a plastic bag."

"Wait..." I tilted my head, pointing at Naomi. "Aren't you the same person who loves to enforce 'the clothes' rule? It's the whole reason why I left in the first place."

"Context matters!" she huffed, throwing her hands up. "The rule applies to ain't shit men who couldn't remember your name during sex or those who don't bother to wash AND dry your clothes after inviting your ass over! This man let you stay the night and cuddled with you. He told you he wanted to talk to you in the morning."

"He kind of said 'later—"

"Semantics, semantics," she rolled her eyes. "Anyways, there's a difference between folded clothes because they're shoving you out the door and folded clothes because maybe they're, I don't know, trying to acknowledge you as a human being with basic decency."

"Okay, but—"

"Nah," she shook her head. "Don't 'okay but' me. You're telling me you didn't even wait for an explanation of what the hell happened this morning? Not even a text? Why didn't you call me so I could've told your ass to wait until he got back?"

I hesitated, chewing on my lip again because I could've called her, but I chickened out. That pause was enough for Naomi to throw her hands up again, looking like she was about to reach through the screen and throttle me.

"Ooooop," Elizabeth leaned back in her chair with a smirk, pointing knowingly at Naomi. "There it is. Naomi patented the '*I'm so done with you*' face. She's about two seconds from blowing up your phone with voice notes ranting for the next hour."

"Unbelievable. Absolutely unbelievable," Naomi shook her head in mock defeat. "You better not have blocked his number, too."

"I didn't block him," I muttered defensively, crossing my arms over my printed bathrobe. "I just... I didn't get his number."

Alexandra squinted at the screen like she was trying to decipher whether or not I actually had any brain cells left. "You what?"

"I—"

"So, let me get this straight—again—just for clarity," she said slowly, her tone dripping with sarcasm as she rubbed her temples. "You ran out of there without saying anything, didn't even get his number so you could call him for clarity now that there's a chance you might be wrong, and you're on the phone with us expecting us to...what? Tell you that was the right move?"

"It felt like the right move at the time," I shot back, my voice higher than intended. "It—"

"You're really making me side with Mimi when she's the one we need to put in time-out half the time," Alexandra cut in, shaking her head.

"Hey!" Naomi scowled. "I'm the only voice of reason around here!"

Elizabeth snorted loud enough to rattle her speaker. "Oh, please. The last time you gave Allie's little sister relationship advice, she ended up keying her man's car and crying in a Wendy's parking lot."

"I did what I had to do," Naomi shot back, narrowing her eyes at Elizabeth through the screen. "And besides, she said she felt liberated! Her words, not mine."

"Back on topic because y'all not about to piss me off and remind me about Charlie's breakdown," Alexandra waved both hands in a calming gesture, her voice smooth and level as always. "All of this is beside the point. The real issue here is communication—or lack thereof. I mean, seriously, girl, you didn't say a word?"

"No," I muttered defensively, though the heat creeping up my neck betrayed me. "I just left once I saw the clothes..."

"Nah, bruh. Your bitch ass ran," Naomi deadpanned. "You slipped out of there faster than Liz cancelling plans when it rains."

"Mimi!" Elizabeth threw her hands up in mock offense, though the smirk tugging at her lips betrayed her amusement. "Chill out!"

"Yeah, Mimi," Alexandra gave her a quick glare. "I know you're right and all, but you're doing the most."

"Look," I said, trying to muster some sort of defense. "I panicked, okay? The whole morning felt...weird. Like get-out-before-you-regret-it-and-have-an-awkward-conversation weird. The clothes were a clear statement."

Alexandra leaned forward again, narrowing her eyes like she was dissecting me under a microscope. "Was it genuinely strange? Or were you simply overanalyzing things like you're used to doing? Or maaaybe, were you just dodging confrontation again?"

Her words hit like a precision strike, and I found myself momentarily speechless, staring at their faces on my screen as if I had been caught red-handed without even knowing I was holding something incriminating. My silence said it all, and Naomi let out a dramatic groan, slapping her forehead.

"Classic avoidance tactic," she groaned. "You don't want to deal with the possibility that it might've been...complicated!"

Elizabeth smirked. "Or that you might've actually liked him."

I shook my head, though the gesture felt weak even to me. "It wasn't like that. I do like him and I was gonna tell him..."

"Then what was it?" Naomi challenged, the tilt of her chin betraying just how much she was holding back. "Enlighten the group. Because from where we're sitting, it sounds a lot like you got scared and avoided conflict once again. You constantly avoided conflict when it came to you and Andrew, letting him do the shit he pulled without ever standing up for yourself until we forced you to face it. And now here you are, different guy, same pattern. This is no different, Sol."

Her words hit harder than I'd anticipated.

The Andrew card.

That was low.

My stomach twisted, and I let out a sharp breath, feeling the hot prickle of defensiveness spike in my chest.

"That's not fair," I said quietly, gripping the edge of my desk as if grounding myself would stop the upheaval in my head. "This isn't like Andrew."

"I don't want to say it but..." Alexandra sighed, "...it kind of feels like Andrew all over again. Not that you're the same person you were back then—you've grown a lot—but some habits are harder to break than others."

"It's not the same," I mumbled, though my voice was weak enough to make me question if I believed myself.

Elizabeth, on the other hand, stayed silent and sipped on her iced coffee.

"Oh, it's not?" Naomi leaned forward, resting her chin in her hand. "Because it looks pretty damn similar from over here. You've got this pattern—you shut down and walk away instead of facing what you're feeling. You did it last night when you saw Andrew with homegirl from high school. Instead of confronting him for lying to you about wanting to get back together, you acted like you didn't care and chose to hang out by the bar until Des showed up."

"That's not the case—"

"Then what did happen, Sol? Huh?" she pressed, leaning so close to her phone camera that her face took up the entire screen.

"Mimi," Alexandra chimed in, her motherly tone shining through. "Let her—"

"Nah," Naomi cut Alexandra off with a wave of her hand. "Nah, Allie. If we keep coddling her, she's just gonna keep pulling this shit. Sol needs to hear it straight for once, and your way of handling things isn't doing what it needs to do right now."

Alexandra released a breath like she was ready to start cursing. "Naomi, don't–"

"I oop!" Elizabeth took another long sip from her iced coffee, her eyes flicking between the three of us like she was watching an episode of Bad Girls Club. "This is getting good," she muttered under her breath, which earned her a glare from Alexandra, which Elizabeth responded with an exaggerated shrug before raising her cup in mock surrender.

"Can I speak now?" Naomi turned her attention to Alexandra who was looking at her like she would smack the shit out of her.

Sighing, Alexandra pinched the bridge of her nose before giving Naomi a begrudging nod. "Watch your words, though. I know I want Sol to move on and find the love she deserves, like we all do, but that doesn't mean you're allowed to bulldoze her into oblivion with your 'tough love' nonsense. Some things require patience."

"Patience, I don't have anymore soooooo," Naomi's death stare bore into the screen as she stared at me. "Sol, what was so terrifying this morning that you couldn't even stick around for a conversation? Hmm? The man dicked you down so good. He was attentive to your needs, he was observant—shit... he was everything you've always wanted in a man and he wanted y'all to talk things out when you weren't tired. Why couldn't you stick around to ask *why* he folded your clothes like a goddamn housekeeper?"

"Jesus...." Alexandra dragged her hand across her face. "I said no bulldozing."

"I'm asking the right questions," Naomi shrugged, turning back to me. "Sol, answer the questions. Cause why couldn't you wait to ask him anything instead of making up a story in your head and bolting? I never knew you to be this scary, so what is it?"

The pause stretched thick between us.

Even Elizabeth, who normally would've taken the chance to add some snarky commentary, stayed silent as she watched me squirm under Naomi's unyielding gaze.

"I..." I hesitated, the memory of waking up in that soft bed washing over me like a tide I wasn't ready to relive. "It wasn't—he wasn't there, okay? The bed next to me was empty. And then there were these...clothes all folded like... It just felt off."

Naomi scoffed. "So you decided to run without getting answers because that's easier than risking—what? Actually hearing something that might challenge the subtle narrative you've already written in your head? Come on, Sol. Do you even hear yourself right now?"

I inhaled sharply, gripping the edge of my dresser until my knuckles blanched.

The subtle narrative you've already written...

Naomi wasn't wrong, and that was the worst part of it all.

She knew me too well.

They all did, and no matter how much I tried to twist or deflect, I couldn't escape the unnerving truth: I had done it again.

I convinced myself I understood the entire situation when, in reality, I'd run before anything could challenge the illusion. That's what I did with Andrew whenever he cheated, which led to our *breaks.* I built this perfect little story in my head where I was unbothered, where it didn't matter because I had already won by not letting him see me crack.

But Naomi was right—I wasn't unbothered.

I was shattered, but instead of standing firm and demanding answers, I let the cracks grow until everything broke beyond repair.

And now, here I was again.

Same broken pieces, different man.

"Maybe I just didn't want to get hurt again," I finally muttered, the words tasting bitter on my tongue. "Maybe it's easier to assume the worst than to..."

"...be vulnerable," Alexandra finished, her eyes kind but filled with that gentle, motherly look she always seemed to have. "I get it now. You're protecting yourself. I really get it because I do it too sometimes. But... running doesn't actually protect you from anything—it just postpones the inevitable, and I don't want you to repeat the cycle you've worked so hard to break out of."

Elizabeth set her coffee down with a clink, tilting her head slightly as she spoke up for the first time in a while. "Look, I understand that it's scary, but you can't just keep running every time something feels off. You kept telling my ass not to run when things started off weird between my man and I… So why aren't you taking your own advice? Weren't you the same person who said *everything suspicious isn't a red flag waiting to slap you in the face*?"

I let out a shaky laugh, but it faded quickly as their words settled into my chest.

Vulnerability wasn't just uncomfortable; it was terrifying. It was a wide-open door begging for heartache, waltzing right in and wrecking me all over again.

To know that Desi had the power to break me scared me more than I'd ever admit to them. I could still feel the ghost of his arms around me, the warmth of his chest against my back as he'd held me. For one night, I'd let my guard down, and the weight of that realization was suffocating.

"Do you honestly believe he would've hurt you after what you told us about him?" Alexandra's question was gentle, yet it wrapped itself firmly around my fraying thoughts. Her dark eyes searched mine through the screen, and I hated how easily her words found the parts of me I wanted to hide.

"I don't know," I shrugged, pretending to adjust my sports bra as if fidgeting with fabric could distract me from the truth.

"Did he even say or do anything that felt off last night? Anything that would make you think he's some kind of psycho, folding your clothes as his goodbye message?"

"But that's the thing, Allie," my voice cracked as my words came out faster than I intended. "It was so… perfect. Too perfect. Like something out of a stupid rom-com where everything falls apart in Act Three because it was never real to begin with. I mean, who does that? Who folds someone's clothes and lets them sleep in without a care in the world? Especially after what we…" I trailed off, feeling my cheeks heat as flashes of last night threatened to overwhelm me.

"You're overthinking it," Naomi exhaled so heavily I could

practically feel it through the phone. "You can't live your whole life planning for a worst-case scenario that might never happen. You think perfect can't be real. That if something feels good, it must be fake or fleeting. News flash: not everyone is out here trying to play you, Sol."

"Okay, but... am I crazy for thinking folded clothes are weird?" I asked almost desperately, trying to redirect their barrage of truths.

Naomi groaned loud enough to nearly blow out my phone speaker. "Sol—if this is about some damn laundry—"

"Hold on, Mimi," Alexandra cut her off gently, raising a hand like she was mediating a debate. "The clothes are...admittedly odd. I'll give her that, and her feelings are valid on the clothes."

"Thank you," I said quickly, clinging to Alexandra's lifeline like it was the last shred of sanity in this conversation. "See? It's not just me."

Naomi rolled her eyes so hard I thought they might get stuck in the back of her head. "Oh, for crying out loud—Lex, don't encourage this nonsense."

"I'm not encouraging it, but I'm validating her feelings," Alexandra interjected with a calm but firm tone, always the peacemaker of the group. "Sure, Sol overreacted—again—but-"

"There's no buts," Naomi interjected, her voice sharp and unwavering. "This isn't about folded clothes. It's not even about him disappearing before breakfast. This is about Sol running from anything that remotely smells like emotional risk."

I squirmed under the weight of Naomi's words but didn't dare speak.

She wasn't wrong, even if I hated the way it sounded when she said it out loud.

"Here's the thing," she continued, softening slightly as she leaned closer to the camera. "You are allowed to be scared, Sol. We've all been there, so you know we get it. Trusting someone new? That's terrifying after everything you've been through. But fear can't be your compass forever. At some point, you've gotta sit with the uncomfortable and at least try to work through it."

"So what should I do?" I asked, my voice small. It felt like a concession, an admission of defeat, but also—maybe—a tiny crack in the armor I'd built around myself.

"Text him," Elizabeth said immediately, as if it were the most obvious answer in the world, then frowned. "Shit... you don't have his number..."

"Oh lord," Alexandra winced. "That does complicate things a bit."

Naomi threw her hands up in exasperation, pacing across her screen like she was on a stage giving some grand speech. "Of course, she doesn't have his number. Great. Alright, fine. I'll hit up T to see if he can give me his number. You said they were friends, right?"

I nodded.

"Perfect. I'm texting him now," Naomi already started tapping furiously on her phone.

"Wait, wait!" I protested, holding up my hands as if that could stop her through the screen. "Mimi, don't! That's so—so embarrassing."

She stopped mid-scroll to glare at me. "Embarrassing? What's embarrassing is you running out of there like a chicken with no head and not doing anything about it for hours. This—" she gestured dramatically at the screen—" is called damage control."

"I don't know if I want to—"

"Too late," she interrupted, tapping her screen with finality. "Message sent. Now we wait and pray to God answers my text. You lucky I'm not letting you wallow in your own mess."

A groan escaped my lips as I flopped back onto my bed. "This is why I don't tell you guys things."

"Please," Elizabeth said with a smirk, crossing one leg over the other on her dark brown office couch. "Who else would keep you accountable? That's what we're here for."

"To be fair," Alexandra added gently, "You needed someone

to push you. Be lucky Mimi didn't do the usual and chose a sane route like texting T for Desi's number."

"Fine," I pouted, staring up at the ceiling, the weight of their well-meaning intervention pressing down on me. "But if this all goes horribly wrong, I'm blaming you guys."

"Blame away," Naomi said breezily, holding her phone up to admire her freshly manicured nails. "As long as you actually grow a backbone out of this, I'll take the hit every time. Besides, you're not gonna regret talking to him—you're just afraid of what he might say."

"Or what he might not say," Elizabeth added pointedly. "There's always that possibility, too."

"Liz!" Alexandra groaned, shooting her a disapproving glare through the camera.

"What? I'm just keeping it real like Mimi did!" Elizabeth replied with a shrug and an unapologetic sip of her coffee. "We all got our reasons for fighting for Sol to fix this."

I sighed, my shoulder slumping as I felt the weight of their words settle over me.

"I gotta get dressed for pilates," I muttered, mostly to escape the suffocating intensity of their intervention. "I'll call you guys later."

Naomi narrowed her eyes suspiciously. "You better not ghost us, Sol. We're in this now."

"Yeah, yeah," I waved her off, standing up to stretch. My joints cracked audibly, and I grimaced, rubbing the soreness out of my shoulders. "I'll text you."

"You better," she shot back, wagging a perfectly manicured finger at the screen before disconnecting the FaceTime call with dramatic flair. Elizabeth and Alexandra muttered their goodbyes as the screen went dark.

For a moment, the room was silent—save for the gentle humming of my overhead fan. My chest felt heavy, like their words were coiled there, refusing to leave me even after the conversation ended. The folded clothes flashed through my mind again—the neat creases, the precise corners—and the way they'd filled me with that gnawing sense of unease.

Maybe it wasn't about the clothes; Naomi was probably right about that much.

But it felt like it was about them.

They represented something bigger—a shift I wasn't ready to confront.

And eventually... I'd have to because I liked Desiderio.

A lot.

15 / DESIDERIO

"Bro," Chance tsked through the phone screen. "I'm starting to think you the problem."

I sighed, taking a seat on my couch. Phone in hand so I could continue the video call, I mentally scrolled through the last couple of hours of my life, searching for evidence to either confirm or deny his accusation.

Having stepped out to grab some food for Solène and me from the bodega down the block, I was shocked to come back to an empty apartment. I had left her to catch up on sleep—after we didn't go to bed until nearly 4 AM— while I grabbed us some coffee and bacon, egg, and cheese rolls. Antonio had the best beef bacon on the block, and I wanted her to try it before she hiked back up to Brooklyn.

But when I returned, her side of the bed was made... and all traces of her were gone.

No note, no explanation... nothing.

The shit rubbed me the wrong way because I had finally made up my mind about her.

About us.

About what I wanted this to be. I spent so much time stuck in my own head last night, questioning every move, every word, every feeling that seemed too big for how new this thing between us was, I had finally landed on something solid.

Something real.

Everything with Solène felt right—Complete, like a jazz song that found its rhythm in a room full of chaos.

She was the notes I didn't know I needed.

The melody that slipped in unnoticed but lingered long after.

I was ready to chase that tune.

To let it guide me through every room, down every street, into whatever murky, rat-infested corners life threw.

I was ready to tell her I wanted to explore something deeper with her.

Yet she never gave me the chance to say my peace.

Or worse, maybe she wanted last night to be a one-time thing while I... again wanted more from someone who didn't.

"I'm not the problem," I muttered, though even as the words left my mouth, they felt hollow. Chance raised an eyebrow, his skepticism practically radiating through the screen.

"Okay," he chuckled, dragging out the word in that annoying way that irked me. "Then what happened? It sounds like you rushed her into something she wasn't ready for."

Me?

Rushing someone into something they weren't ready for? *Nah.*

"How's that possible? I was patient with her, I listened, and I thought we had a good night together based on.... No, I *know* we had a good night together and I didn't rush shit," my voice dipped into frustration. "And then she... left like all of it meant nothing. We didn't even get to talk about it."

"You sure you ain't miss any signs?"

I opened my mouth to retort but snapped it shut just as quickly.

Signs...

Had there been signs? Sure, Solène had her moments where

she pulled back, moments I observed where she seemed like she was more comfortable skating the surface than diving into deeper waters—but wasn't that just her being cautious?

Didn't I show her that caution wasn't necessary anymore?

"I don't know," I leaned forward, rubbing a hand over my face in exasperation.

"That's your problem right there," Chance jumped in, smirking slightly. "You don't know, no matter how observant you are. Sometimes, these women are showing you things in ways that aren't wrapped up with a nice little bow. Gotta pay attention, man."

I groaned, slumping into the couch. "So now I'm supposed to be some mind-reading detective or something? Come on, man. That's not realistic. It's like... what happened to just talking? Saying what you mean instead of playing all these damn games?"

"Women are complicated, bro," he threw his hand up in mock surrender. "They protect themselves and move on their own accord. Hell... Half the time, they don't even know what they want until they're halfway down the road, looking back at you, wondering why you didn't run after them."

I let out a bitter laugh, shaking my head. "That's supposed to make me feel better? That she doesn't even know what she wants?"

"I didn't say it was supposed to make you feel better. I'm just saying maybe this isn't all about you. Maybe she's the problem."

I stared at the screen, letting Chance's words settle like dust in the endless clutter of my thoughts.

The problem wasn't me?

I wanted to believe him, but the knot in my chest told a different story.

The Solène I got to know was layered, intricate. She was a blend of contradictions—confident yet guarded, playful yet full of hesitations. That's what drew me to her in the first place: the depth, the layers she didn't wear on her sleeve but hinted at with every subtle glance, every unfinished sentence.

But… maybe I'd mistaken those openings for something more permanent.

Maybe those glimpses weren't invitations to stay… just warnings that I was getting too close.

Maybe… and I hated myself for the thought crossing my mind… *Maybe I'm not enough.*

Maybe I was never enough for a woman to stay long enough to take me seriously. Maybe that's why I still hadn't been in a relationship after all these years of half-starts and almosts. Maybe I was the kind of guy women kept around for a good time, but never for the long haul.

The thought burned deep in my chest, a toxic swirl of confusion and disappointment I couldn't shake.

All I wanted was to be enough for someone.

Enough for them to stay, enough for them to trust me with their chaos, enough for them not to see me as just a temporary fix.

But no matter how much effort I put in, how much I tried to show up as the man they deserved, it always seemed like I fell short.

I stared at the bag of food I'd brought back; it probably wasn't even warm anymore.

Talk about a fucking metaphor.

"Stop that shit," Chance said. "You're doing it again."

"Doing what?" I bit back, though I knew exactly what he meant.

"That self-blame shit. I was joking about you being the problem earlier but you're taking that shit to heart."

"I'm not—"

"I'm watching you spiral in real time, bro. You do it everytime you think you meet someone you think could be the one and my jokes aren't hitting because you're too busy digging a fucking grave for yourself. Listen, Des, every time something doesn't go your way with a woman, you start pulling out the microscope, looking for ways to blame yourself. You ever think maybe it's just not about you?"

“Maybe… but it’s hard not to when I watch my friends find their happily-ever-afters while I’m stuck replaying the same damn pattern,” the words slipped out before I could stop them. Sinking further into the couch, I murmured, "I try to do everything right. I can’t help but feel like I’m the common denominator, man. Like maybe I’m just… defective.”

Chance let out a long, exaggerated sigh, the kind he always used when he thought I was being particularly dense. “Bro, you’ve got to stop tying your worth to whether someone else sticks around or not. That’s not how this works. You think everything’s a checklist—do this, say that, show up like this—and then boom, you’re golden. But people? Man, they don’t operate on your timeline or logic. Especially women.”

I squeezed the back of my neck and stared off at the corner of the room, guilt crawling over me. I hated how much his words made sense while still managing to make me feel like utter shit.

“And another thing,” he continued before I could gather myself for a response. “You ever think maybe she left because she’s dealing with her own shit? Like maybe it’s got nothing to do with you? Sometimes folks leave ‘cause that’s how they survive—not ‘cause you fucked up or aren’t good enough.”

“But she could’ve said something,” I argued weakly. “A note… anything.”

“True,” he leaned back in his chair, his face softening as he stared at me through the screen. “She could’ve said something. And yeah, maybe she should’ve. I ain’t giving her a pass for ghosting you like that ‘cause its fucked up. But you—” he pointed, his finger nearly poking through the phone’s camera, “you can’t sit here tearing yourself apart over it. Not every storm gotta be your fault.”

I sighed, staring at the untouched coffee on the table in front of me.

“I know you’re right,” I said slowly, forcing myself to meet his gaze. “But let’s just pretend for a second that I missed something. I brought her over to my house—”

"You what?" His eyes widened. "Woah woah woah, run that back. You did WHAT?"

"She... came over?"

"You brought her over to your house? I thought y'all kicked it at a hotel, but your place??"

"Yeah—"

"You're joking, right?" he took a dramatic pause, his fingers pressing against his temples. "Des... Bro. Your house? Like, your space-space? Like YOU brought her into your space when you've never brought anyone to your spot before? The guy who keeps his crib locked up like it's a CIA black site suddenly opening doors for some girl you just met??"

I hesitated, my thoughts colliding like bumper cars. "Yeah, I brought her over. We were soaked from the rain last night, so I invited her back to dry off, warm up, you know—the whole shebang. We talked, we... yeaaaaaah... and in the morning, I folded her clean clothes and left them on the chair in my room while she was sleeping—why's your face like that?"

My friend's jaw dropped, and for a moment, he just stared at me like I'd confessed to robbing a bank. Then he burst out laughing—a loud, obnoxious guffaw that echoed through the phone speaker.

I frowned. "What?"

"Bro... bro..." he choked out between wheezing laughs. "I can't believe you're this stupid. Everything makes fucking sense now!"

"What? What I do?"

"You, oh my God," he shook his head in disbelief. "You basically told her ass to politely get the fuck out in girl code. You're over here bitching and self-destructing—the shit my therapist says I be doing sometimes—when you folded her clothes like it was some farewell gift!"

I blinked at him. "Wait... Coño, what are you even talking about? I cleaned up her stuff and went out to get us food. How is that 'get out' energy?"

He wiped tears from the corners of his eyes, still grinning like he had caught me in some cosmic joke. "Bro... folding clothes? Leaving them on the chair? You practically said bye."

"But I put it by my clothes so she wouldn't think that she was some kind of guest or something temporary. How the hell does that translate to an exit strategy?"

"You're missing the point. It's not about what you meant; it's about what she saw. Women are hyper-aware of shit like that. You could've put her clothes back in a drawer with yours, or just left them where they were—but noooooo, you folded 'em real neat and set them off to the side. That's like saying *Here's your stuff all prepped for you to grab whenever you're ready to dip cause I don't want you here*. Like a concierge at a hotel checking her out without asking if she wanted to extend her stay."

My fingers raked through my hair as I sat there, stunned.

So I wasn't the problem, but if what Chance was saying was true, then I might've accidentally become the problem.

Mierda.

"Women notice everything," he continued. "They connect dots we can't even see because we don't think like them. To you, it's just folded clothes on a chair; to her, it's a farewell note in origami. I did that to my girl one time and got my ass cussed out 'cause she thought I was trying to put her on a timer."

I buried my face in my hands, groaning into my palms.

"I just... I wanted her to be comfortable."

"Yeah... comfortable leaving," he snorted. "How the hell do you have two sisters and you—"

"Don't," I looked back up, my eyes turning into slits. "Cali's eighteen and Ana's in middle school. Both of them haven't had a one night stand to tell me what the fucking etiquette is for post-rainstorm hookups."

He shook his head in amusement. "Doesn't take a genius. If you leave anything open to interpretation, girls like Solène will fill in the blanks with their own wild conclusions."

I narrowed my eyes at him. "Don't need to rub in my mistake. I already know I screwed up."

"First off," he smirked like he'd just scored the game-winning point. "I'm not done with you so buckle the fuck up."

"You're seriously enjoying this too fucking much.."

"Yeah, I am 'cause if it was me? I wouldn't have folded her clothes like I work retail. That's mistake number one. You wanna make someone feel at home? You don't itemize their existence into a neat little square of folded fabric and leave it in the 'guest zone.' You blur the lines, Des. Toss her stuff somewhere casual. Hell, let it mingle with yours—make it look like you're already living in a world where she belongs."

I scoffed, but his words planted seeds of doubt and realization that sprouted uncomfortably fast. The more I replayed the scene in my head, the more I saw how badly I fucked up.

"Alright, alright—"

"I ain't done negro." he went on without missing a beat, "Mistake number two, you fucked up by not leaving a note. You just dipped without saying anything and expected her to magically know you were coming right back?"

"I was gone for like eight minutes..."

"And those eight minutes was all she needed to rewrite the story in her head."

"That's insane," I murmured, though the certainty in my voice had started to unravel. "She would've known—she *should've* known—that I wasn't trying to get rid of her. I mean... it was obvious we had something good last night."

He raised an eyebrow.

"Damn it," I finally relented. "Shit... Okay, so what do I do now? She's gone. Just like that. I don't have her number."

He echoed with a raised brow, tilting his head as if the answer was so obvious it shouldn't even need to be asked. "Go after her."

"How the fuck am I supposed to do that?"

"Talk to Tone instead of talking to me."

“I tried, but he’s not answering.”

“Then figure it out, bro. I can’t help you with that one."

I sighed, glancing around my apartment like the answer might be hiding in one of the corners.

"Man, this is ridiculous," I muttered under my breath, but even as I said it, I found myself standing up. My keys were on the counter where I’d tossed them earlier; I grabbed them without thinking.

"I don't even know how to find her," I snapped, though my feet were moving toward the door anyway. I froze for a second, hand on the knob.

Where the hell was I even planning to go?

Go to Brooklyn on a hunt for her?

What if... she didn’t want me to find her? What if leaving like that was her way of closing the door, of making sure no further steps were taken?

I hesitated, keys clinking softly in my hand.

The weight of uncertainty pressed down on me, grinding against the hope I didn’t want to admit I still had.

All of this felt so raw, so messy, and I hated how much it mattered to me.

Maybe I should make peace with the fact that she *chose* to leave.

“Des,” Chance’s voice carried through the phone, dragging me out of my spiraling thoughts. “Don’t stand there overthinking. You’ve got two options: sit your ass back down and let this shit eat you alive until you regret it for the rest of your life, or you get out there and try to fix it, regardless of what happens. Either way, bro, make a damn decision.”

The line went quiet for a second as I stood frozen in place, my hand tightening around the doorknob. My chest felt tight, split between the fear of rejection and the hope that maybe—just maybe—I could fix this before it was too late.

Chance let out an exaggerated sigh. “Look, Des... I know you’re scared. I get it, man. But fear don’t mean shit if you let it win every time. You want her? Prove it. You already said she ain't got a clue how much you care. Now's your shot to show her."

"And what if she doesn't want me to?" I muttered, my throat tightening as the words came out.

"Then at least you'll know."

16 / SOLÈNE

PILATES WAS the last thing on my mind.

Though I dressed the part, I found myself unable to attend the noon class with a clear mind... Which led me to wander aimlessly through the park on Bedford Ave. The summer heat pressed down on the back of my neck like an unwelcome hand as I walked, coaxing beads of sweat along my hairline. The air was thick with the smell of freshly cut grass. Children shrieked as they chased each other around, their laughter an almost mocking contrast to the heaviness in my chest.

The world moved around me, but my brain was focused on Naomi's words.

Fear can't be your compass forever. At some point, you've gotta sit with the uncomfortable and at least try to work through it.

I thought I had done the part where I sat with the uncomfortable.

I had attended therapy after Andrew and I finally called the quits, I halted dating until I was sure I wasn't dragging old baggage into something new, and I... I...

A bitter chuckle escaped my lips as I shook my head.

I lied to myself that I was.

The truth? I'd been using movement—literal and figurative—as an escape. Pilates, DJing, and surrounding myself with my friends to not feel alone for the past year... They were shields dressed up as self-care. I used them as distractions from sitting still long enough to feel any real discomfort. I avoided the quiet moments like they were landmines, terrified of what might detonate if I stepped too close. Stillness meant reflection, and reflection meant I'd have to confront the truth lurking beneath the surface—the truth I'd been so meticulously dodging.

I was afraid of what I'd find if I stripped everything away.

If I peeled back the layers of curated progress, would there be anything solid underneath?

Or was I just a hollow shell I'd painted over with bright colors and called it healing?

I stopped walking.

Sinking onto an empty park bench, the slats felt warm against my back. Around me, life continued: joggers darted past with their headphones in, and a dog barked insistently at a squirrel just out of reach. The world was utterly indifferent to my spiraling and, in some perverse way, that felt like its own kind of relief.

I pushed a curl out of my face, trying to will my thoughts into submission, but they resisted.

They always did.

Sitting here now felt too close to what Naomi had challenged me to do—sit with the uncomfortable. My fingers fidgeted against the bench as if grabbing for something else to focus on, something physical to anchor me against the swell.

And yet... What was I running from?

What was this nebulous *fear* that kept me from clutching onto movement like it was a lifeline?

My chest tightened as I wrestled with the question, my breath shallow and uneven. Suddenly, a song with similar undertones played from a jogger's wireless speaker as they passed. Though it was different, it summoned the song I now hated because it came with the memory of Andrew. The melody curled around my thoughts like a predator stalking its prey. I gritted my teeth against it, but the lyrics bubbled up anyway, dragging me back to that final moment of us in his car while we drove through Flatbush—the one where I realized all the things I had hoped for with him were nothing but fumes.

I just don't think this is working anymore, Andrew's voice—low and monotone—slipped into my thoughts uninvited. The memory was so vivid that I could almost smell the orange of his cologne mix with the heat of the park. My hands tightened into fists against my thighs as the scene replayed, unrelenting.

"You don't think this is working?" I'd repeated, hollow and disbelieving, staring out the window at the familiar streets blurring by. We'd passed Larry's Deli, where we used to grab sandwiches after late nights out, and yet there he was dismantling everything we'd built like it was nothing more than an expired lease.

His silence then had said it all. His grip on the steering wheel was too tight, his jaw clenched as if saying anything more would somehow justify it.

He didn't want to fight.

He didn't care to defend his words or soothe the wound they inflicted.

Andrew had already checked out long before that conversation began—I just hadn't seen it.

That realization—his absence in moments where he should have been present—hit me harder than his actual words. And now, sitting on this bench in a park miles away from all that heartbreak, all I could think about was how Desi's small action overlapped in a way that scratched at old scars I thought had healed.

Andrew had been emotionally absent long before he said the words out loud. He had left me to piece together the fragments while his silence did the breaking for him. And maybe, just maybe, that was why Desi's absence and the action of my folded clothes this morning felt like déjà vu.

But it wasn't fair.

Not to him—not to Desiderio, who had shown up for me in

ways Andrew never would have dreamed. I couldn't keep punishing someone new for the sins of someone old.

Yet knowing that and *feeling* it were two separate things.

Logic didn't quiet the storm inside me; it only made me feel guilty for standing at the center of it.

My hands stilled against the bench as the realization settled in.

If I wanted to break the cycle, I had to be brave enough to name my own ghosts. I had to admit to myself that I was now the problem. My fear wasn't of heartbreak or loneliness or even failure. It was staring too long and too hard at whatever version of myself existed after all the distractions faded away. I didn't want to see her—not really.

Because what if she wasn't enough?

What if the person I'd fought so hard to become over the past year wasn't anyone at all?

The thought hit like a gut punch, leaving me breathless for a moment.

What if I'm not enough?

A sharp wind picked up, tugging at my shirt and teasing my hair into my face, and I let it happen—let myself feel it instead of smoothing it away like I normally would. The restless part of me wanted to stand again, to walk or stretch or even run until my legs burned enough to drown out everything else, but I stayed planted on that bench.

At some point, you've gotta sit with the uncomfortable and at least try to work through it.

So I stayed until the discomfort wasn't bothersome anymore.

17 / DESIDERIO

THE SMARTEST THING would've been to wait for Tony to hit me back up.

Abuela always told me patience was a virtue, yet here I was in Williamsburg contradicting my better judgment.

Chasing a possible clue about Solène's whereabouts, I was like some feen chasing their next fix. I knew better than to act the way I was acting, but desperation had a way of rearranging my boundaries.

I refused to repeat the pattern of having another fling not work out, leaving me holding a bag full of regrets and "what ifs."

I refused to listen to a constant narrative where I wasn't enough for someone to stay.

Not this time.

Not with her.

So yeah... I was out here in the fucking heat of Brooklyn, sweating bullets through my shirt as the sun beat down on me like it had a vendetta. However, it was better than sitting at home replaying our last moment for the thousandth time.

"Did the noon class already finish?" I asked the brunette dressed in bright pink at the white counter.

Yun's Pilates was the first place I started digging. While it wasn't much to go on, it was worth checking out.

"You're looking for someone specific?" she teased, her voice dripping with something else I didn't have time to unpack. Giving me a once-over before sensually biting her lip, she leaned forward, her bright blue acrylic nails tapping an uneven rhythm that matched my rising impatience.

Was she trying to... *Breathe, Des.* ***breathe.***

"Yeah," I nodded, ignoring the way her eyes looked at me like I was her meal. "I was hoping to catch her before she went home."

"Oh," she purred. "You sure you're not just here to see me?"

"I'm sure."

She tapped her nails again like she was savoring the moment as she looked at me over again. Seconds—or what felt like hours passed before she finally let out a breathy laugh, shaking her head.

"Did it end or—"

"Noon class just ended about fifteen minutes ago," she finally said. "If your friend was here, she's already gone. Most of the girls leave pretty quickly... unless they're hanging around for the juice bar or whatever." She gestured vaguely toward the other side of the street, where a small crowd gathered near a neon sign flickering *Refuel.*

I clenched my jaw, biting back the urge to snap for having wasted my time. Instead, I nodded curtly.

"Thanks."

Her lips curled into a smirk, as if my frustration amused her. "You sure you don't want to leave your name or... I don't know your number? In case I see her?"

Ignoring the blatant invitation in her tone, I shook my head. "I'll take my chances."

The smirk faltered for just a second before she shrugged and leaned back from the counter, clearly deciding I wasn't worth more of her time.

Good.

I had enough distractions to deal with.

Got a juice bar to check out.

Of course, it couldn't be this easy.

I spent my entire afternoon checking every potential business around the pilates studio that gave the vibe Solène might stop at.

The juice bar? A bust.

The little artisan bakery two doors down? Nada.

A vegan café down the street? Useless.

Even an artsy little shop two blocks over, with vinyls, turned out to be nothing but a waste of precious time. Williamsburg was turning into a maze of dead ends, each one mocking me for thinking I'd find her so easily.

If Abuela could see this right now... she'd be laughing her ass off, shaking her head and muttering something about me being a fool for chasing after someone like this.

But papá would've nodded—he always said a man should fight for what matters to him, no matter how foolish it might look to everyone else.

And right now? She mattered.

The sun was starting to dip low, painting the sidewalks in gold as my stomach growled its protest for the last thing I ate was some coffee and a baconegg&cheese. People buzzed around me, wrapped in their own lives. Tony still hadn't answered my calls—probably 'cause he was either high or trying to sleep off last night's festivities.

I checked my watch, frustrated that I spent four hours wandering a part of Brooklyn I barely knew for a clue that probably didn't exist.

Four hours chasing fantasmas.

I should quit and go home.

Pack it up and admit that Solène—for now—was a phantom I wasn't catching.

I was operating on fumes and needed more than blind hope to get anywhere.

Cursing under my breath, I opened my phone to call for a ride home. I was ready to give up, but my screen lit up with a call, Tony's name flashing across it like some cruel cosmic joke.

Gracias, Madre Mía.

Remind me to light a candle for you later, I swiped to answer faster than a broke man catching a dollar in the wind. "Took you long enough, perra."

"Fuck you too," came Tony's scratchy voice on the other end, clearly still half-asleep. I could hear faint music in the background—some reggaeton track echoing through wherever he was. "The fuck you call me so many times for? You in trouble or something?"

"You got Naomi's number?" I asked, cutting straight to the point. "I need it."

He paused for a second, maybe longer, giving me that telltale silence that meant he was either thinking too hard or about to give me shit. "You calling me like it's life or death just for Naomi's number? You serious right now? On top of that... no hi or hello?"

"Don't piss me off. I've been trying to get ahold of you all day, pendejo."

"Fine, fine," He groaned, the sound strained and heavy, like I'd just asked him to move a mountain. "But why Naomi? Why the hell you looking for her number—wait... is this about her friend, Solène? Cause I seen that Naomi texted me a couple of hours ago asking for yours. Something about her friend. Y'all looked cute together last night."

Wait... Naomi wanted my number for Solène?

Was she trying to reach out to me, too?

My stomach flipped, hope sparking like a faulty lighter. For a moment, I stood frozen in the middle of the crowded Brooklyn sidewalk, my mind racing as I processed my best friend's words.

Could this finally be the break I was looking for?

"Yo, Des. You still there?"

"Yeah... She texted you?"

"Maaaan," he said, his voice still groggy. "She was all like, *Oh, can you send me his number?* She didn't give me much more detail than that, but I could tell she was serious 'cause she usually ghosts me for days before texting back about anything. This was the first time I've seen her hit me up that many times in an hour."

"Please tell me you sent it to her." I was going to lose my mind if he hadn't followed through.

"Nah, I figured I'd check with you first," he said, dragging the words in that lazy drawl of his. "Didn't wanna just hand it out like that, y'know?"

"Jesús," I hissed. The heat slapped me again like a disapproving abuelita's chancla, but I barely felt it over the tight coil of frustration winding in my chest. "You could've solved this hours ago??"

"Vato, slow down," He yawned loudly, the sound crackling through the phone like static. "I just woke up. Besides, how was I supposed to know it was urgent? Not like you sent me a heads-up or anything."

I pinched the bridge of my nose, crossing the street to dodge a group of teens on skateboards. "I'm gonna smack the shit out you. I called like six times!"

"Aight, main, Aight. Calmate," he muttered, sounding more amused than concerned. "I'm on it. Hold your damn horses."

I heard faint clicks as he typed—agonizingly slow.

"You sent it yet?" I snapped, already mentally chewing through the seconds he was wasting.

"Patience is a virtue, hermano," he drawled lazily, finishing with a loud tap of his screen. "And... done. Naomi's got your number now. Happy?"

Relief punched through my chest like a sledgehammer, loosening the knot of tension I'd been carrying all day. I was finally close to my answers—or at least a lead. "Finally. You're almost useful for once."

"Yeah, yeah," he said, stifling another yawn. "I expect a thank-you in oxtail pizza next time we hit up that spot in Bed-Stuy."

"Don't hold your breath," I tucked the phone back into my pocket, ignoring the growing heat on the back of my neck.

Did Solène tell Naomi about last night?

Is that why she's looking for me?

The questions swirled in my head, colliding and twisting until they tangled into an impossible knot.

But what if— I sighed, and shook off the brew of doubts before they could settle.

What-ifs wouldn't get me anywhere.

Neither was standing here in the middle of the street. It was better to go home than to let my mind wander in circles. If she really wanted to talk, then I'd hear from her soon enough. Running around like this—winding through endless blocks, chasing nothing—I was just wearing myself out.

Reaching into my pocket again, I pulled out my phone to check Uber prices and winced at the surge fare.

Typical.

Looks like I'm doing the train.

Shoving my phone back into my pocket, I crossed the street to enter the L subway station. I could already feel the nasty heat of the subway platform wrapping around me like a simmering stew. The stale air underground was somehow worse than the street, clinging to my skin and making every step feel heavier. I grew restless, my fingers brushing the edge of my phone screen like I could will it to buzz with a message from Naomi. The train wasn't due for another six minutes, and every second dragged like I was stuck in molasses.

Finding a pillar to stand against, I leaned back and stared at the pavement across the tracks, my mind spinning faster than the approaching train could ever go. Sweat trickled down the back of my neck in salty rivers, clinging to the edge of my white shirt. The screech of an incoming service announcement crackled overhead, but I barely registered the garbled voice. My focus tunneled into the black void beyond the tracks, where faint yellow headlights flickered.

Five minutes left.

My hands itched to check my phone again—just to make sure I hadn't missed something in those moments since Tony's call. Logic told me Naomi couldn't have sent anything this fast. Hell, she might not even be next to her phone right now. Yet the raw, stubborn part of me refused to accept that waiting patiently was my only option.

Four minutes.

My legs flexed, my shoulders twitching as commuters around me floated in and out of the station like people living lives I couldn't touch or care about. A man in a Yankees cap drifted by holding a duffel bag that smacked someone's shoulder, generating a stream of muffled curses. A couple argued quietly near the stairs —her arms crossed defensively over her chest, his fingers twitching midair like he wanted to reach for her but didn't know how. A rat scurried across the tracks as the eerily familiar screech of another train echoed deeper into the tunnels.

Three minutes.

The train lights grew brighter now at the end of the tunnel. My hand moved against my better judgment, lifting my phone from my jeans pocket to check yet again. No missed calls. No messages. Nothing but a blank notification screen mocking me.

I cursed under my breath and shoved it back in place. Staring wouldn't make anything happen. Still, Naomi's text—or lack thereof—had my thoughts spinning into endless theories. Did Solène change her mind before reaching out? Did Naomi forget that Tony sent her my number? Or worse, did something happen that none of us could've planned for?

Two minutes.

The air shifted as the approaching train churned it into a warm gust. Around me, commuters began drifting closer to the edge of the platform, positioning themselves without thought or care about what might come next in anyone else's world.

Just monotony.

Steps to follow and routines that would reset tomorrow like clockwork.

One minute.

The lights of the train grew blinding as it rounded the bend, the sound of its grinding wheels rising. My chest felt tight, every heartbeat echoing with an impatient thrum that matched the rhythm of the train's approach. It wasn't just frustration anymore. It was the heat, the noise, the weight of waiting for something I couldn't control. I thought about skipping it—letting this train come and go while I paced this sticky, filthy platform like some idiot waiting for answers from a line that might never call back.

However, what would that solve?

Another twenty to thirty minutes until another train crawled through, and then what?

More standing around like a dumbass?

No. I'd get on, head home, and let Naomi do whatever she needed to do.

Solène could make her move if that's what she wanted.

Her friend had my number now.

The screeching brakes screamed louder as the train came to a halting stop in front of me. Doors hissed open. People pushed against each other with nonchalance as they filed in and out like cattle—heads down, eyes glossed over, thoughts hidden behind AirPods or cheap knockoffs.

And then, just as I stepped forward to board, a flash of terracotta hair caught my eye through the shifting bodies on the other side of the platform. My breath hitched with a sharpness that felt like swallowing chivo picante down the wrong hole once the person turned—because there she was.

My Butterfingers.

18 / SOLÈNE

1289 Lexington Ave.

Staring at the address in the history of my Uber app, I contemplated whether I was truly about to do what I was thinking about. Though this was the next step that I needed to take after confronting the uncomfortable parts of me, I was still chickening out.

Sitting in a park alone with your thoughts was a lot easier than facing the man who I wasn't sure I even had the courage to confront. It wasn't just the fear of what he might say—it was the fear of confirming what I already suspected deep down: that I'd ruined something fragile before it even had a chance to bloom.

And the thought of him looking at me with that same mixture of pity and exasperation, Andrew always tossed my way? That was enough to make my stomach twist into tight knots as if it were preparing to implode.

Yet I continued to stare at the address again.

Ready to close the app, a call from Alexandra came instead. I hovered over the green button for a moment before answering, steadying my breath like it might make me sound less on edge.

"Hey," Alexandra's voice came through calmly. "You okay?"

I exhaled, leaning back against the park bench as I stared up at the trees swaying gently in the breeze. Their movement felt soothing—a contrast to the storm brewing inside me.

"Define 'okay,'" I said with a weak laugh, trying to inject some humor into my voice.

"You're thinking, aren't you?"

My jaw clenched as I debated denying it, but what would be the point? "How did you know?"

"Lucky guess," she countered with a knowing tone that made me want to roll my eyes. "We've been best friends since middle school, so I know you, Sol. Also, Mimi texted me five minutes ago saying, 'I betchu Sol sitting somewhere overthinking her life right now instead of showing up to Desi's door and talking like a normal human being.'"

Damn you, Naomi.

Groaning, I let my head fall back against the bench. "Of course she did."

"She's not wrong," I could feel my best friend smile over the phone as if she could read my mind. "But she's also not entirely right. You don't have to do this if you're not ready."

"I don't know if I'll ever feel ready... I don't even know what I'd say to him."

"Is this your way of asking me for help?"

"I—I guess so."

Alexandra sighed, her silence stretching just long enough to make me wonder if the call had dropped before she finally spoke again. "You say the truth. As messy and uncomfortable as it is, you just... tell him how you feel."

"What if..." I let out a shaky breath, pulling my knees up to my chest as I balanced the phone against my ear. "What if he doesn't want to hear it? What if he tells me that I'm not..."

"Enough?"

Her words filled the silence I couldn't bring myself to break. It was like she had reached into my chest and yanked out the one thought I was too scared to voice.

"Yeah," I whispered, the word barely audible, but Alexandra caught it.

"If that's what you're so afraid of, then maybe he's not the right person for you after all. But Sol... What if he does want to hear it? What if he doesn't think that at all? What if you find out that he's been sitting on the other side of this whole scenario, wondering why you left?"

I swallowed hard, her words cutting through me in a way that left no room for denial.

"You've spent all this time imagining what could go wrong," she continued. "But have you even dared to imagine what might go right?"

"I—"

"I know you've been through hell with Andrew—trust me, I do—but not every man is going to treat you like he did. And from everything you've told us about him, Desi doesn't strike me as the type to walk all over you without a second thought. So, you owe it to yourself to stop assuming the worst and give it a real chance."

"But.... you didn't see how perfectly folded the clothes were, though..."

"I didn't," she quietly laughed. "But I also know you're like me when it comes to romance. We both self-sabotage at the first sign of vulnerability." She paused, letting her words simmer before continuing. "What if this is different? What if you're wrong about what those folded clothes actually meant? What if instead of being a closure, they were... I don't know, assurance?"

"Assurance? How can that be assurance?"

"Sometimes actions—small, insignificant actions—carry more weight than anything words could say. Maybe folding your clothes was his way of showing care without waking you up or imposing on your rest. Not every gesture has to read like a novel, Sol. Some people speak in little things. You just have to listen differently."

I let her words sink in as I traced the edge of the Uber app on my screen with my thumb.

"I—" I furrowed my brows as her words took root in my mind, causing me to close the ride-share app. "I gotta go, okay?'

"Text me later," she said. "And Sol?"

"Yeah?"

"You're braver than you think."

I hung up before I could respond with something snarky or let her kindness unravel me completely. For now, I needed to focus—to block out doubts, fears, and the nagging little voice that sounded an awful lot like Andrew at his worst.

Quickly opening the maps app on my phone, I looked up which train line would take me back to Desi's. The J train seemed the most direct, though it required a switch at Broad Street. I could also walk to the L, and it would cut down my commute by two to three minutes.

I bit my lip, tapping my phone against my thigh, knowing time wasn't the real issue at hand.

The thought of returning to his apartment, to the scene of my self-made chaos, was what made my stomach churn.

But the thought of not returning, of leaving things unsaid and unresolved, was worse.

So with a deep breath, I stood up and opted for the J train on Marcy Ave to cut down the nerves. The L felt too close to cheating, and I deserved the extra minutes of contemplation as I rehearsed what I'd say.

I'm sorry for leaving. No.

I'm a mess, and you deserve better. C'mon, Solène.

Maybe I should just start with, *Can we talk?* Simple. Direct.

It left room for him to choose whether or not to even engage.

That seemed fair, right?

Fairness wasn't exactly my strong suit lately, but maybe this was a good place to start.

"Butterfingers!"

I froze.

It couldn't be.

My heart leapt into my throat as I turned. At first, I couldn't locate the source of the voice amidst the sea of commuters roaming the platform, but then as I continued looking? My eyes found him on the other side of the platform with a couple of teenagers. His hands in the air, waving exaggeratedly like he was flagging down a plane, there stood Desiderio. He was dressed in a plain white t-shirt and black shorts, his dark hair a tousled mess. For a second, I thought my mind was playing some cruel trick on me.

Maybe I had willed him into existence with nothing but guilt and wishful thinking.

But then he smiled—that sharp, crooked grin that always seemed to toe the line between charm and trouble—and yelled. "Don't move! I'm coming to you."

I blinked.

Before I could so much as process his words, he was already jogging toward the stairs of the opposite platform, weaving through the crowd with hastiness. A train rumbled in on his side of the station, its screeching brakes briefly drowning out the chaos in my chest, and for a moment, I lost sight of him.

I took a step back, clutching my phone like it was a lifeline.

What was he doing here?

This wasn't his neighborhood—not even close.

And why now, of all times, when I'd finally summoned the courage to face him on my terms?

My legs itched to bolt down the platform and onto the waiting train like some invisible cue had just sounded an alarm.

But before I could act, there he was again—emerging from behind a cluster of commuters, leaning heavily against the stair railing as if he'd run a marathon. His breath came in audible bursts by the time he reached me, hands bracing his knees as he glanced up with that same grin that disarmed me far too many times before.

"You... you," he panted between breaths. "You left and.. I was... Jesus."

"I was what?" I asked, my voice sharper than I intended.

Fuck, not a great way to start.

However, I didn't know how else to sound.

My heart was hammering, my brain ricocheting between confusion and that annoying flicker of hope I was desperate to swat away.

He straightened, his chest still heaving as he pressed one hand against it.

"I was trying to figure it out," he said finally, his grin fading into something softer, something almost unsure as his eyes searched mine. "You left without saying anything. No note, no text, just... gone."

I looked away, searching the platform for something to look at, but everything my eyes landed on redirected me right back to him.

"I thought you wanted me to leave," I said quietly, my lips dry as they formed the words. "I saw the folded clothes and—"

"That was a mistake. I shouldn't have left them out like that. It wasn't... it wasn't what you thought."

I frowned, the noise of the subway tunnel around us dimming as his words sank in. "Then what was it?"

"I didn't think much of it," he rubbed the back of his neck. "I took your clothes out of the dryer, folded them and left them next to mine to get us breakfast. I thought you'd still be there when I came back, and... you were just gone." His voice cracked. He stepped closer, his face shadowed but his dark eyes relentless as they locked onto mine. "Solène, I didn't want you to leave."

I opened my mouth to reply, but nothing came out. My mind was cycling through fragments of memories, still trying to realign what I'd perceived that morning with what he was saying now. The clothes, freshly laundered and perfectly folded, had seemed like such a glaring signal at the time.

"So..." I began, my voice soft and uncertain now. "You weren't... trying to push me out?"

He ran his tongue over his bottom lip before exhaling hard through his nose. "Push you out? Nah. I have no idea how you got that from anything I did. If anything..." He faltered for the first time since we'd laid eyes on each other again, his gaze lowering to the grimy subway platform with a vulnerability that caught me off guard. "If anything, I was trying to find a way to ask you to stay longer. I was gonna tell you that... I didn't want it to just be a one-time thing. That I wanted more than... whatever that night was."

The air suddenly felt too thick in my lungs, too heavy against my skin. My mouth opened, but nothing came out. My mind scrambled through fragments, trying to realign what I'd seen that morning with what he was saying now.

I had run.

Not just from him, but from the possibility of something real.

My friends were right.

I was a goddamn coward.

The weight of it hit me like the wind of yet another train pulling into the station—a sudden, undeniable truth barreling toward me with no chance to dodge. I had let fear drive the narrative, let assumptions fill the gaps where honesty should have been.

And now here he was, laying everything bare while I fumbled for a response that could bridge the gulf between us.

"Desi," I finally managed, his name leaving my lips like an unpracticed word. "I didn't know... I thought I—" I stopped myself, frustrated at how small my voice sounded, at how inadequate every explanation felt.

"You thought what?" he asked gently, stepping closer still until we were only a breath apart. His tone had softened, but there was something behind it that made my throat tighten. "That I'd fold your clothes and pack you out the door like it meant nothing? You really think I'm that kind of guy?"

"I don't know what to think," I admitted. The words rushed out before I could stop them, stinging with more emotion than I'd intended to reveal. "I didn't know what any of it meant! You folded my clothes, Des. I know that sounds stupid, but for a second, it felt like a goodbye. And I've had enough of those—"

His hands were suddenly bringing my face gently upward, his palms warm against my cheeks as he interrupted my spiraling.

"Stop," he said quietly, his voice steady but kind, like he was trying to anchor me. "Stop overthinking for just one second."

My breath caught in my throat.

The noise of the subway station faded into a hum. Around us, the chaos blurred into oblivion. His dark eyes locked onto mine. There was no avoiding him now, no looking away, no running.

His gaze held me there, pinned me in place, and for the first time in forever, I felt completely seen.

"You didn't know what any of it meant because I ain't say it," he continued, his thumbs brushing against my skin in soft, absent circles. "I should've told you—should've made it clearer with a note instead of some folded laundry. But you've got to know by now what I've shown you all night..." He hesitated for a heartbeat, his jaw tightening before his next words came out low but firm. "... I don't do things halfway. I never have and never will."

I swallowed hard, the lump in my throat refusing to budge as his words settled over me like a blanket I wasn't sure I deserved. My instinct screamed at me to look away, to retreat into the safety of deflection, but his hands held me steady, both physically and emotionally.

I couldn't run from this.

Not anymore.

"What are you saying?" I whispered, barely able to hear my own voice over the craziness of the subway station. "That you... that we..."

"I'm saying... I'm saying... I don't know how this is supposed to go, but I know I don't want last night to be the only thing we have."

I don't want last night to be the only thing we have.

My heart thudded painfully against my ribcage.

I stared at him, my cheeks still cupped in his hands, as if trying to discern whether I'd misheard. However, Desiderio didn't falter, didn't shrink back, or let doubt cloud the clarity in his gaze. His words were there, solid and unyielding like a foundation being laid brick by brick.

"But what if I mess it up?" The question slipped out before I could stop it, the crack in my voice betraying just how deeply rooted that fear had grown inside me.

"You might," he smiled down at me. "But that's alright because I might too. You're not the only one who overthinks things."

"And if we both mess it up? What then?"

"Then we try again," he shrugged like it was the simplest answer in the world. Like it wasn't terrifying or impossible or maybe both. His thumbs traced lazy arcs against my cheeks as he added, "I'm not scared of a little mess, Solène. I'm scared of not trying at all."

His hands dropping from my face, he took a step back, giving me space as if to let his words settle.

"So what do you say?"

I stood there, caught between the roaring train and the question lingering between us. My pulse boomed loud enough to drown out every ounce of logic I might have clung to—the part of me that wanted to calculate risks, prepare escape routes, avoid pain.

But logic had gotten me here, hadn't it?

Stumbling through a mess of my own making, unable to say what I truly felt.

I searched his face for something—anything—that might let me off the hook, but all I saw was patience.

That look broke something in me.

It softened the jagged edges I used to shield myself, made me want to be braver than I'd been in years.

"I say..." My voice trembled, but I didn't stop this time. "I say we try."

THE END

EPILOGUE

FIVE MONTHS LATER

"DESSS," I giggled. "I gotta gooooo. They're waiting for me."

Laid up in Desiderio's bed with his head nestled on my bare stomach, he hummed a low, lazy protest. His fingers traced absent-minded patterns along my rib cage as though he were drawing constellations only he could see. His breath warmed my skin, and for a moment, I forgot about the world waiting beyond his bedroom door.

"They can wait," he murmured, his voice thick with sleep. "You're not going anywhere... not yet."

I laughed softly, threading my fingers through his curls.

Some days were always like this—with him—this dangerous pull that made time irrelevant and responsibilities feel distant.

But I couldn't afford to let him win today.

Not this time.

Having just returned from a DJ gig in London three days ago, I assured my best friends that I'd join them for our monthly adulthood brunch recap. Naomi had an important announcement to make, and knowing her? It was bound to be something dramatic.

Besides, I couldn't skip it, especially after avoiding them for the last seventy-two hours, holed up in his apartment like we were both lovesick fugitives.

"I can't," I insisted, half-heartedly. My resolve was crumbling quicker than sugar in warm tea. "I haven't seen the girls in two weeks."

"And you haven't seen me in what? Close to a month now, thanks to work?" he tilted his head to look up at me, pouting. "You owe me some time, too."

"I know, but..."

He pulled the covers over his head and muttered something incoherent.

"Des," I said again, firmer this time, though my resolve wavered as his lips brushed just below my belly button. "Seriously, I have to go. I promise I'll be back."

He groaned, threw the covers off his face, and rolled onto his back, throwing an arm across his eyes in exaggerated defeat. "You're cruel, you know that? You're heartless, mami."

I propped myself up on an elbow, peering down at him. The sight of him naked in his bed, all dazed curls and that maddening pout—he was almost about to make me reconsider brunch entirely. *Almost.*

"Heartless?" I repeated, tracing a finger along the edge of his jawline. "You're the one trying to kidnap me."

He dropped his arm and tilted his head toward me, dark eyes glinting like he was plotting something mischievous. "Is it kidnapping if I don't want my girlfriend to leave?"

Girlfriend.

Still getting used to the sound of that word.

Though it'd been four months since he made a grand gesture to ask me to be official—roses, candles, a playlist of all my favorite songs, and cake that asked the big question—it still made my stomach flip every time he said it.

Girlfriend.

It felt foreign and thrilling all at once, like I'd stumbled into a shiny new reality we were building together.

I rolled my eyes, but my cheeks betrayed me with the faintest warmth. "That's not how it works."

"Pretty sure it is," he countered, pulling me down by the wrist until our faces were inches apart. His grin was wicked, as if he knew exactly how torn I was. He let the silence hang there, his breath brushing against my lips, daring me to close the space between us. My resolve wavered again, my willpower slipping like water through clenched fists. It was unfair, really, how easily he unraveled me with a single look, a single touch.

"You're impossible," I whispered, though there was no venom in the words. They were soft, amused, dangerously close to surrender.

"And you love it," he said, that grin only widening. He kissed me quickly—soft and brief—before pulling back just enough to watch my reaction. His gaze roamed over my face like he was committing every detail to memory and taking his sweet time with it.

I groaned and flopped back onto the mattress in mock defeat, staring up at the ceiling as if it might have answers to my predicament. "You're really making this hard."

"That's the point," he teased, rolling onto his side to prop himself up on one elbow. His curls fell across his forehead in a way that made him look effortlessly perfect in the kind of way people shouldn't be when they'd just rolled out of bed. "What kind of man would I be if I let you leave without a fight?"

"A decent one?" I offered, glancing sideways at him.

"Nah," he drawled, leaning closer until his face hovered just above mine. "Ain't no fun in being decent."

He bent closer, his lips ghosting over the curve of my cheek, stopping just shy of my ear. His voice dropped, smooth and low. "...and you don't date decent men, Butterfingers. You date me," he finished with a grin that I could hear in his voice as much as I could see in my mind's eye when I closed them.

I rolled my eyes again, though my body betrayed me by leaning slightly into him.

“Fine,” I stuck my tongue out at him, reaching for my phone to text Naomi and the girls that I’ll be late. “Ten more minutes.”

He grinned. “Ten minutes, huh? Bet.”

Before I could protest—or clarify that my ten-minute allowance didn’t mean ‘open season’ on my self-control—he moved. Quick as a cat, he shifted his weight over mine, pinning me beneath him. His hands braced on either side of my head as he looked down at me, his curls dangling like soft shadows.

“I’ll make those ten minutes worth it,” he whispered, leaning down until his lips left mine.

Yeah... I never stood a chance.

“Okay, nooooow I gotta go,” I said as I slipped on my light blue jeans, shimmying them up my hips while he lounged back against the headboard, watching me with a self-satisfied smirk. He looked infuriatingly pleased with himself, all stretched out like a lazy orange cat who’d just demolished a third meal that wasn't even his to begin with.

“Now?” he crossed his arms, smirking. “You sure you don’t need another ten minutes?”

“I’m sure,” I grabbed my folded turtleneck from the seat and tugged it over my head. Catching his eyes lingering, I stuck my tongue out at him playfully, and he let out a low chuckle.

“Suit yourself,” he said, stretching his arms above his head, the sheet slipping down to reveal more of that golden skin. “Buuuut you gonna be thinking about me all through brunch.”

“I think I’ll survive,” I quipped back, knowing it was a lie, slipping into my leather puffer coat.

“Brave words, Butterfingers,” he mused, reaching for his drawer on the bedside table. “Let’s see how long they hold up.”

I grabbed my bag from where it hung on his bedroom chair

and slung it over my shoulder. He didn't look up, but I could feel his attention on me like a simmering heat. As much as I loved the way he watched me, it was dangerous—it made leaving harder than it needed to be.

As I reached the bedroom door, his voice stopped me.

"You forgot something."

I turned, scanning the room. "What?"

He slipped into a pair of white Yankees sweats lying on the ground and padded towards me, a hand behind his back. Ready to ask what he was hiding, he pulled his hand forward, revealing a small box.

My breath caught, and I blinked at the box in his hand—small, square, and wrapped in glossy black paper with a gold ribbon tied neatly around it. The sight of it silenced whatever smart-ass reply had been forming on my tongue.

"What..." I managed to croak, my voice barely above a whisper. "Des... what is that?"

He didn't answer right away. He just shrugged one shoulder.

"Des..."

"Open it," He held it out to me like it was both casual and sacred, and I hesitated for half a second before taking it. My fingers brushed his in the exchange, electricity sparking where our skin connected—he had that effect on me, even after all this time.

I turned the box over in my hands.

"What is this?" I asked again, quieter this time.

His arms crossed over his chest as he leaned against the doorway, his face unreadable. "Open it."

I untied the gold ribbon, the silky texture slipping through my fingers, and carefully peeled back the black wrapping paper. My heart thudded as I opened the small box, revealing a keycard and a silver key.

Did he just...

"It's for here. Well..." he cleared his throat. "The keycards's for the building, and the other one's to this place... to my place."

Oh shit, he did.

I blinked at him, unsure if my heart was racing from excitement or sheer panic—or both in equal measure.

"I... a key?"

He took my hand into his. "I want to show you something else."

Guiding me back into the room, we stopped in front of his dresser, a modest oak piece covered with his usual clutter—his designer watch, a half-empty bottle of cologne, a few forgotten coins.

"What are you—"

He opened the second drawer down, and I gasped.

"I..." he rubbed the back of his neck. "I know it's kinda soon, and the last time we talked about it was when we were joking around and all but... I-I made some room for you."

Inside the drawer, half of it was completely empty. The other half held a handful of my things—small, familiar items I hadn't even realized I'd left behind. A silk hair tie, a tube of my favorite lip gloss, and one of my favorite scarves from the night we had a wine picnic on his balcony. My black Prince hoodie that I thought had disappeared two months ago was neatly folded.

My throat tightened at the sight, warmth pooling in my chest despite myself. He must have gathered them piece by piece, quietly storing them away without saying a thing while he waited... for what?

Me to notice?

The right moment?

"I—uhm..." he started, running a hand through his curls in that telltale way he did when he was trying to play it cool but failing miserably. "It's just a drawer. You don't have to like... move in or anything. I just figured—y'know—you always leave stuff here anyway and you're here so much so why—I don't know—I thought it'd be... nice for you to have some stuff here so you can feel more at home when you're here," He trailed off, his voice softer now. "My mamá loves to say that a man's space says more about him than his mouth ever can, so...uhm... yeah..."

I stared at the drawer, then at him, then back at the drawer.

My fingers tightened on the keycard and key in my hand, the metal pressing into my palm like an unspoken question.

A drawer.

A key.

His place.

He had made space for me—not just physically, but in his life. For the past five months of us being together, Desi had been so full of surprises, equal parts playful and intentional. He'd put his heart into everything in ways that always left me breathless.

But this?

It surpassed the court-side seats to the Yankees game—

No... this was right up there with the grand gesture of asking me to be his girlfriend.

Though it was done casually, this was him saying, without actually saying it:

You belong here.

With me.

My chest tightened, like every emotion I'd buried was rushing at me all at once. It was overwhelming in the most beautiful way, and I suddenly didn't care if Naomi and the others would tease me later for being late.

"Des..." I raised my eyes to meet his. I didn't even know what I was going to say; the words still formed formless shapes in my head. However, before I could finish—or stumble over the explanation—he leaned in and kissed me.

The kiss wasn't a playful, teasing kind of kiss he'd been giving me all morning or the ones that tasted like temptation.

This one was something else entirely.

It was steady, unhurried, full of unspoken promises and careful intention. His lips moved against mine like they were planting roots, quiet promises blooming in places words couldn't reach..

My fingers curled instinctively into the front of his shirt—*God, when did he even put one on?*—and I let myself fall into it for just a moment longer than I should have.

When he finally pulled back, his forehead rested against mine, his hands sliding down to lace with my own.

"You don't have to say anything," he whispered, his voice barely audible. "I just... I just wanted you to know, even though we haven't been with each other that long. I really like you and I want you to feel at home here and—"

"I know," I finished for him. My free hand stayed curled in his shirt as if letting go might make the moment evaporate into thin air. "I know, baby."

His forehead stayed pressed to mine, and for a few heartbeats, neither of us moved. His hands squeezed mine gently, and though he didn't say anything, I could feel it—everything he wanted me to understand but couldn't put into words.

I stepped back slightly, just enough to look up at him fully. His dark eyes searched mine for some sign—whether for reassurance, acceptance, or something else entirely, I didn't know.

But what I did know was that he'd opened a door I hadn't even realized we were standing in front of.

And as I stood there, clutching that small, carefully presented key in one hand, it hit me—this wasn't just about a drawer or a keycard or even his apartment.

This was about the space he'd carved out in his world for me, the way he shifted his life to make room for mine.

It was something bigger.

Something scarier.

Something I hadn't let myself fully think about until now.

I used to run from this kind of thing, yet I knew without a doubt that today... I wanted to walk through that door.

"Okay," I said, my voice steadier than I expected. His brow lifted in question, his lips parting as though he was about to ask what I meant, but I didn't give him the chance. "Let's do it. The drawer. The key. All of it."

His arms tightened around me reflexively, pulling me closer, as if he thought I might take the words back if he let go too soon.

"Yeah?" his voice tinged with disbelief, the cocky confidence from earlier melting into something softer, more vulnerable.

"Yeah," I whispered back, letting out a breath I hadn't realized I'd been holding.

His smile grew slowly, wide and bright like morning sunshine creeping across the room. And there it was—his whole heart written on his face for me to see without a single guard up.

"So... a drawer, huh?" I teased softly after a moment, hoping to lighten the weight that threatened to steal my voice. "You give a girl a whole drawer and a set of keys? Bold move."

The corner of his mouth twitched upward into that cocky smirk I'd come to both love and curse. "What can I say? I'm generous like that."

I laughed, lightly swatting his arm. "Generous, huh? That's what we're calling it?"

"That's exactly what we're calling it."

"Well," I tilted my head to look at him through narrowed eyes. "I guess I could find a few things to keep in that drawer. Maybe."

"Really?"

"Really," I stood on my tiptoes to press a quick kiss to his cheek before stepping back. "Okay, now I gotta go."

"Yeah, yeah," he sighed dramatically, releasing my hand but not before brushing his thumb against my palm one last time. "Go be a good friend. Save me some gossip for later."

"Deal," I said, grinning at him as I slipped the keycard and key into the inside pocket of my leather bag. I couldn't stop the giddy warmth that spread through my chest every time I thought about them resting there—a tangible piece of him I was taking with me.

Out in the building hallway, I glanced back to find him leaning against the doorframe, watching me go with that familiar, crooked grin, his arms casually crossed over his chest. "Oh, and Butterfingers?"

I paused mid-step, raising an eyebrow. "Yeah?"

"Don't forget," he said, voice dropping to that velvet tone he reserved for moments like this, "Come back home to me."

My heart skipped a beat at the sound.

Come back home to me.

"I will," I called back, pressing for the elevator button. "I promise."

FOR MORE DESI & SOL:

To read more of Solène and Desiderio's love journey as it continues to progress, feel free to join my patreon for more exclusives and behind the scenes content.

- Olive W.

RECIPES FROM READY OR NOT

For those who are interested in experiencing some of the foods that have been mentioned in this story... here's your opportunity to try them. These recipes carry my own personal touch—each one infused with the same heart, heat, and hunger that lingered between the characters. These dishes aren't just meals; they're memories. Moments stirred into saucepans, longings baked into crusts, stories simmered over low heat. If you've ever wanted to taste a little of the love shared on these pages, now is your chance.

Makes: 4 servings

Prep Time: 10 minutes

Cook Time: None

Chill Time: 30 minutes (optional)

Total Time: 10–40 minutes

Equipment

- Blender
- Fine mesh strainer (optional, for a smoother drink)
- Pitcher
- Serving glasses

Ingredients

- 2 cups fresh or frozen cherries, pitted
- ½ cup freshly squeezed lemon juice (about 3–4 lemons)
- ½ cup sugar, honey, or sweetener of choice (adjust to taste)
- 2–3 cups cold still or sparkling water
- Ice cubes
- Lemon slices and whole cherries, for garnish

Instructions

0. **Blend the Base**

In a blender, combine cherries, lemon juice, sugar, and 1 cup of the water. Blend on high until smooth.

0. **Strain (Optional)**

For a smoother texture, pour the mixture through a fine mesh strainer into a pitcher, pressing to extract as much liquid as possible. Discard solids.

0. **Dilute and Adjust**

Add the remaining cold water (still or sparkling) to the pitcher. Stir well. Taste and adjust sweetness or tartness as desired.

0. **Chill and Serve**

Refrigerate for 30 minutes, or serve immediately over ice. Garnish with lemon slices and whole cherries.

Tip: For a refined twist, replace half the water with sparkling water just before serving for a refreshing fizz.

Makes: 10–12 empanadas

Prep Time: 30 minutes

Cook Time: 30–40 minutes

Assembly & Frying: 30–40 minutes

Total Time: Approx. 1.5–2 hours

Equipment

- Large skillet or sauté pan
- Mixing bowls
- Fine mesh strainer
- Cooling rack or paper towels
- Frying thermometer (recommended)

Ingredients

Empanadas

- 10–12 six-inch empanada wrappers
- Canola oil, for frying
- 10–12 slices provolone cheese (optional, or use a milder cheese like mozzarella)

Seafood Filling

- ½ lb raw shrimp, peeled, deveined, chopped
- ½ lb lump crab meat (drained if using canned)
- ½ cup bell peppers, finely chopped
- ¼ cup red onion, finely chopped
- ¼ cup green onion, sliced
- 1 small carrot, peeled and finely diced
- 1 jalapeño, deseeded and finely chopped (adjust to taste)
- 1 tablespoon garlic, minced
- 1 tablespoon ginger, minced
- 1 teaspoon dried oregano
- 1 teaspoon allspice (optional, for Caribbean-style warmth)
- 2 tablespoons green seasoning (or mix of cilantro, garlic, scallion, and lime juice)

• ¼ cup heavy cream or coconut milk (for moisture and richness)
• 1 tablespoon tomato paste or ketchup
• Salt and black pepper to taste
• 1 tablespoon canola oil
• Optional: splash of white wine or fresh lime juice

Optional Dipping Sauce (Simple Citrus Aioli)

• ¼ cup mayonnaise
• 1 teaspoon lime juice or lemon juice
• 1 garlic clove, grated
• Pinch of salt and pepper

Instructions

Prepare the Seafood Filling

0. Heat 1 tablespoon oil in a skillet over medium heat. Add bell peppers, onions, carrot, jalapeño, garlic, and ginger. Cook for 3–5 minutes until softened.

0. Add chopped shrimp and cook for 2–3 minutes, until just pink.

0. Stir in crab meat, green seasoning, oregano, allspice (if using), tomato paste or ketchup, and cream or coconut milk.

0. Simmer gently for another 2–3 minutes until mixture thickens slightly. Season to taste with salt, black pepper, and a splash of wine or lime juice if desired.

0. Remove from heat and cool completely before assembling.

Assemble and Fry the Empanadas

0. Place an empanada wrapper on a clean surface.

0. Optional: Lay a slice of provolone or mozzarella cheese in the center.

0. Add about 2 tablespoons of seafood filling.

0. Optional: Top with another small piece or half-slice of cheese.

0. Fold the wrapper over to form a half-moon shape. Seal the edges firmly and crimp with a fork.

0. Heat canola oil to 350°F in a deep pot. Fry empanadas in batches for 4–5 minutes, or until golden brown and crispy.

0. Drain on a cooling rack or paper towels.

Optional Dipping Sauce

In a small bowl, mix mayonnaise, lime juice, garlic, salt, and pepper. Serve alongside the empanadas if desired.

Serves: 4

Prep Time: 20 minutes
Cook Time: 3 hours 30 minutes
Total Time: 3 hours 50 minutes

Ingredients

Smoked Oxtail:

- 4 lbs oxtails
- 2 Tbsp browning sauce
- 1 Tbsp oxtail seasoning
- 1 Tbsp kosher salt
- 1 Tbsp neutral oil
- 1 carrot, peeled and chopped
- 1 bell pepper, chopped
- 1 onion, chopped
- 3 scotch bonnets
- 1 Tbsp garlic, minced
- 1 Tbsp ginger, minced
- 3 sprigs fresh thyme
- 1 Tbsp oxtail seasoning (additional)
- 2 Tbsp ketchup
- 2 Tbsp soy sauce

For the Pizza:

- 2 Tbsp Thai sweet chili sauce
- 1 prepared pizza crust (defrosted if frozen)
- 1 cup shredded mozzarella cheese

Pro Tip:

If you can't find oxtail seasoning, combine:

1 tsp each of garlic powder, onion powder, paprika, cayenne, allspice, dried thyme, and turmeric.

Instructions

1. Smoke the Oxtail

- Toss oxtails with browning sauce, oxtail seasoning, and salt until fully coated.
- Place oxtails in a single layer inside a smoker preheated to 250°F.
- Smoke for 1.5 hours. The meat should be cooked through but not fall-off-the-bone tender yet.

2. Braise the Oxtail

- In a large Dutch oven over medium-high heat, add the oil.
- Sauté the carrot, bell pepper, and onion for about 5 minutes, until softened.
- Add scotch bonnets, garlic, ginger, and thyme. Cook for 1–2 minutes, until fragrant.
- Stir in ketchup, soy sauce, and the additional oxtail seasoning.
- Add the smoked oxtails to the pot and cover with water.
- Bring to a simmer, reduce heat to low, cover, and cook for 1.5 hours until the meat is fall-apart tender.

3. Prepare the Oxtail Topping

- Remove oxtails from the pot and discard the bones.
- Shred the meat and place it in a mixing bowl.
- Stir in the Thai sweet chili sauce until the meat is fully coated.

4. Assemble & Bake the Pizza

- Preheat oven to 500°F.
- Spread the seasoned oxtail over the pizza crust.
- Top with mozzarella cheese.
- Bake on the bottom rack for 15–20 minutes, until crust is golden and cheese is bubbling.
- Let cool slightly, slice, and serve.

LA MELODIA

A vibrant raspberry-blueberry sparkler with subtle sweetness and a deep sunset hue.

Equipment

- Cocktail shaker
- Fine mesh strainer
- Tall glass or flute

Ingredients

For the Cocktail:

- 1 cup crushed ice
- 1½ oz chilled vodka (plain or blueberry vodka)
- 4 Tbsp blueberry-raspberry simple syrup *(see below)*
- 3 oz sparkling water or soda water
- ½ oz grenadine
- Squeeze of lemon (optional, for brightness)
- Fresh blueberries and raspberries (garnish)

For the Blueberry-Raspberry Simple Syrup:

- ½ cup blueberries
- ½ cup raspberries
- ½ cup sugar
- ½ cup water

Instructions

1. Make the Simple Syrup

- In a small saucepan, bring blueberries, raspberries, sugar, and water to a gentle boil.
- Simmer for 5–7 minutes until berries break down and syrup thickens slightly.

• Strain through a fine mesh strainer, then cool completely before use.

2. Shake the Cocktail

- Fill your shaker with crushed ice.
- Add vodka, 4 Tbsp simple syrup, and lemon juice if using.
- Shake vigorously until well-chilled.

3. Build the Drink

- Strain into a glass with fresh ice.
- Top with sparkling water.
- Gently pour in grenadine to create a beautiful layered effect.

4. Garnish & Serve

- Float a few blueberries and raspberries on top.
- Serve immediately and enjoy the taste—and the view.

Makes: 10–12 empanadas
Prep Time: 30 minutes (plus marinating time)
Cook Time: 2.5–3 hours
Assembly & Frying: 30–40 minutes
Total Time: Approx. 4 hours (plus marinating)

Equipment

- Large pot or Dutch oven
- Mixing bowls
- Tongs
- Fine mesh strainer
- Cooling rack or paper towels
- Frying thermometer (recommended)

Ingredients

Empanadas

- 10–12 six-inch empanada wrappers
- Canola oil, for frying
- 10–12 slices provolone cheese

Oxtail Filling

- 3–4 lbs oxtails
- 1 cup bell peppers, chopped
- ½ cup red onion, chopped
- ½ cup green onion, chopped
- ½ cup carrots, peeled and chopped
- 2 jalapeños, deseeded and finely chopped (adjust to taste)
- 7–8 sprigs fresh thyme, tied with kitchen twine
- ½ cup green seasoning (Caribbean-style or homemade)
- 1 tablespoon ginger, minced
- 1 tablespoon garlic, minced

- 1 tablespoon dried oregano
- 1 tablespoon allspice powder
- 2 tablespoons browning
- 2 tablespoons brown sugar
- 1 tablespoon salt
- 1 tablespoon black pepper
- 1 tablespoon canola oil
- ½ cup ketchup

Creamy Sweet Chili Sauce

- 1 cup sweet chili sauce
- ¼ cup mayonnaise
- 1 tablespoon soy sauce

Instructions

Make the Creamy Sweet Chili Sauce

0. In a bowl, whisk together the sweet chili sauce, mayonnaise, and soy sauce.

0. Mix until smooth and fully combined.

0. Refrigerate until ready to serve.

Prepare the Oxtail Filling

0. **Marinate the Oxtail:**

In a large bowl, combine oxtails with bell peppers, red and green onions, carrots, jalapeños, thyme, green seasoning, ginger, garlic, oregano, allspice, browning, salt, and pepper.

Mix thoroughly, cover, and marinate in the refrigerator for 24 to 48 hours.

0. **Sear and Braise:**

- In a large pot over medium heat, add 1 tablespoon of canola oil and the brown sugar.

• Stir constantly until the sugar melts and turns a light caramel color.

• Remove the oxtails from the marinade (reserving the liquid) and sear in batches until browned on all sides.

• Deglaze the pot with the reserved marinade. Return all oxtails to the pot and add enough water to just cover the meat.

• Stir in the ketchup. Cover and simmer on low heat for 2 to 3 hours, until the meat is fall-apart tender.

0. **Shred the Meat and Reduce the Sauce:**

• Remove the oxtails from the pot, discard the bones, and shred the meat.

• Skim excess oil from the cooking liquid.

• Bring the liquid to a boil and reduce until thickened.

• Return the shredded meat to the sauce and stir to coat. Let cool before assembling.

Assemble and Fry the Empanadas

0. **Prepare the Wrapper:**

Place a 6-inch empanada wrapper on a clean surface.

0. **Add the Filling:**

• Lay one slice of provolone cheese in the center.

• Add about 2 tablespoons of the oxtail filling over the cheese.

• Top with a second small piece or half-slice of provolone.

0. **Seal:**

Fold the wrapper over to form a half-moon shape.

Press the edges to seal and crimp with a fork.

0. **Fry:**

• Heat canola oil to 350°F in a deep pot.

• Fry empanadas in batches for 4 to 5 minutes, until golden brown and crispy.

- Transfer to a cooling rack or paper towels to drain.

Serve

Serve the empanadas hot with the creamy sweet chili sauce on the side or drizzled over top.

ACKNOWLEDGMENTS

They say it takes a community to raise a child—turns out, it also takes one to birth a book full of heartfelt slow burn moments, questionable decisions, and at least eight rewrites because I didn't know what I was doing half of the time.

To my Alpha Readers — Shoshona, Asia, Raquel and Oona: You guys read this thing in its most unhinged form and still told me this story was worth it. You saw the chaos that an emotion evoked and said, "Yes, I want more of that. Gimme more." I will forever cherish you for accepting my rough of roughest drafts and I owe y'all some empanadas for the rollercoaster ride you went through.

To my Beta Readers — Layna, Natalie, Allie, and my brother Ace: You caught the typos I was too emotionally attached to and pointed out the things I was pretending didn't exist. Special thanks to Ace for reading his little sister's romance novel without combusting or spamming my phone to tell me how nasty of an individual I am (I'll take the Zane compliment you texted me). That's true love.

To Anya, my language whisperer: Thank you for keeping my Spanish grammar in check and saving me from misspelling things. Thank you for your accuracy on Dominican men and their mannerisms. Without you, Desi would've been lacking some of his special tricks.

To Tasha, my editor: I would like to start off by thanking you for believing in me long before you read this book. You gave this story the breath of air it needed with your edits. You made this story sharper, cleaner, and so much better than it started. You're forever stuck with me now *evil laugh*.

To Mia, thank you for assisting me with the title. I had a hard time choosing one b/c this book was never meant to exist (it was a draft I wrote to process a heavy therapy session) but you found the perfect title.

To the six year old me who didn't know English was going to be her third language, you did it. Reading the dictionary and thesaurus in English finally paid off. Your ESOL classes finally paid off. You wrote your first book in a language that you once didn't know.

And to everyone else who helped bring this story to life—thank you for believing in it, and in me. Now let's never speak of how many drafts this took and move onto the next story because it's only getting crazier from here.

WHAT'S NEXT?

Book Two of *The Nape Series*
Coming 2026

ALSO BY OLIVE WINTER

SHORT STORIES FOUND ON OLIVE'S SUBSTACK:

If You'd Stayed a Little Longer

Inspired by A Couple Minutes by Olivia Dean, two exes bump into each other again & spend a half hour taking inventory of what never quite ended.

The Call Before the Moment

Inspired by "Wish I Didn't Miss You" by Angie Stone — here's a late-night call from the man about to marry someone else, and the woman who once believed she'd be the bride.

Open Wide, Sonder

Inspired by "Gimme Some More" by Busta Rhymes, when the woods start calling her name, a camp counselor learns that keeping everyone safe includes surviving her own reflection.